27,515
13.95

JF
LIS

Lisson, Deborah

THE DEVIL'S OWN

DATE DUE

JAN 1 4 1994			

DEMCO

THE DEVIL'S OWN

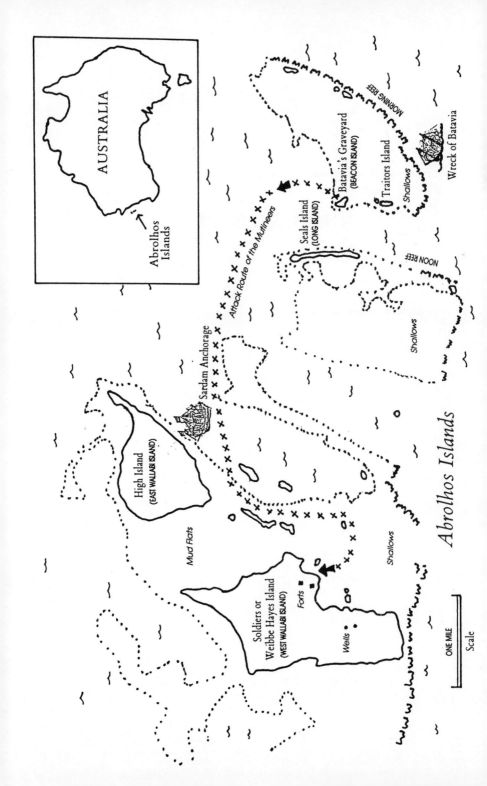

AUSTRALIA

Abrolhos Islands

Wreck of Batavia

MORNING REEF

Batavia's Graveyard
(BEACON ISLAND)

Traitors Island

Shallows

Seals Island
(LONG ISLAND)

Attack Route of the Mutineers

NOON REEF

Shallows

Sardam Anchorage

High Island
(EAST WALLABI ISLAND)

Mud Flats

Shallows

Soldiers or
Weibbe Hayes Island
(WEST WALLABI ISLAND)

Forts

Wells

ONE MILE

Scale

Abrolhos Islands

Deborah Lisson

THE DEVIL'S OWN

Holiday House / New York

First published by Walter McVitty Books, Australia
First published in the United States by Holiday House, Inc., 1991
Printed in the United States of America

Lisson, Deborah.
The devil's own / written by Deborah Lisson.
p.   cm.
Summary: Bored on her father's yacht off the west coast of
Australia, fifteen-year-old Julianna finds herself swept into a
seventeenth-century nightmare of shipwreck, mutiny, and murder.
ISBN 0-8234-0871-X
[1. Time travel—Fiction. 2. Australia—Fiction. 3. Shipwrecks—
Fiction.]   I. Title.
PZ7.L6918De   1990
[Fic]—dc20   90-47106   CIP   AC

Dedicated to
"Sergeant Blake of the Ironfists"
and to
Polyp and all who sailed in her,
Summer 1986–87

We undersigned persons being present on this island, councillors as well as soldiers, sailors as well as our Dominie, no-one excepted whoever it may be, accept as our Chief, as Captain General, Jeronimus Cornelisz, to whom we, with one accord and each separately, swear, so truly as God shall help us, to be faithful and obedient in all that he shall order us; and insofar as the contrary happens, we shall be the Devil's own.

Oath taken by the mutineers on *Batavia*'s Graveyard, 20 August 1629.

1

"*IT'S JUST the moon, skipper,*" *said Hans the gunner. "The reflection of the moon on the water." Aarian Jacobsz grunted and went back to his restless pacing. Moonlight. What else had he expected in the middle of this godforsaken ocean? The heels of his sea-boots struck with an angry sound against the deck. He was sick of this voyage: sick of the wind, sick of the darkness, sick of this interminable watch. His mind wandered longingly to the comfort of his cabin and the warm bunk where Zwaantie Hendricx lay waiting for him. "Not long now," he consoled himself. "Not long and it will all be over. Just play your cards right." He leaned over the bow rail and spat into the ocean. His eyes flickered across the choppy water and suddenly he froze in disbelief. A long, icy tentacle of fear squirmed its way down his spine. "You fool!" he screamed. "You stupid, half-witted imbecile! That's not moonshine, it's* surf!" *He grabbed the wheel from the bewildered steersman and wrenched it round despairingly.*

A rolling breaker lifted the ship and dumped her onto the reef. She struck in a shower of spray and her hull

1

shuddered. There was silence . . . a long suspended agony of horror. Then panic erupted like plague in every corner of the ship. Men, women and children, catapulted from sleep into a nightmare of chaotic terror, stumbled about half blind in the pre-dawn darkness, and clawed and groped their way up to the deck. They screamed abuse at one another, fought like dogs for illusionary places of safety and howled hysterical prayers at an indifferent ocean.

On the deck chaos reigned. Jacobsz was still hurling curses at his lookout. Jan Evertsz, the bosun, bellowed orders to an unheeding crew, and the Commandeur, white faced and weak from his recent illness, was struggling to make his voice heard above the uproar. "What have you done to us?" he shouted at Jacobsz. "God's blood, man, what have you done to us?"

The skipper whirled on him in fury. "I suppose you could have done better. Is it my fault that fool of a lookout can't tell the difference between surf and moonlight?"

Pelsaert choked down his anger; this was not the moment for recriminations. "Where do you think we are?" he asked quietly.

"God only knows. Somewhere off the coast of Eendracht's Land and stuck on a bloody shallows. Stop whining, man. I've been on banks before and got off them. We'll put out a stern anchor and wind her off when the tide rises." He turned to shout for the uppersteersman. "Claas, fetch the lead from your cabin. Let's see how much water we've got round this sodding ship."

The results were not good: little more than three fathoms behind them, almost nothing in front. They put out a boat and sounded further out. A hundred metres or so astern they found seven fathoms. With renewed hope they began to prepare an anchor.

The wind blew harder. The ship floundered in the shallow water like a beached whale and shuddered sickeningly against the reef. The passengers slipped and scrabbled on the rolling deck, screaming with terror. And then the sun came up. For the first time they saw the jagged rocks and the surf boiling all around them. The terrible truth finally dawned on them. A wave of the receding tide ran out beneath the stricken vessel. It surged, swelled and, lifting her again, drove her relentlessly forward. Her bow rose out of the spray and hung for a moment etched against the sky like a wounded bird. Then she heeled over and, with a grinding crunch, embedded herself deep into the coral of Morning Reef.

Julie Dykstra sat on the duckboard of *Salamander*, crumbling stale cake into the Indian Ocean. Beneath her hand the sea bubbled like a cauldron as myriad tiny fish leapt and threshed, stirring the water to a frenzy in their fight for the tasty morsels. Julie watched them in fascination, marvelling at their variety and colour: the lithe elegance of the slender wrasse, the blue and yellow brilliance of the moontails, and the anonymous multitude of tiny, striped fish who flashed through the water in a rainbow of black and white and yellow. They lived around the jetty, these beautiful little creatures, and hung about the sink outlet of the yacht, waiting for scraps. Stephanie spent a lot of her time feeding them; it helped to relieve the boredom and provided an escape from the rest of the family.

She could hear them now, her family, chatting away down in the saloon. She knew exactly what they would be doing. Her parents and aunt and uncle would be playing euchre, Paul would have his nose in a book and Anna and Michelle would be sitting with their heads together, giggling over whatever stupid secrets twelve-year-old girls always shared. Julie considered her sister and cousin with scorn. Babies! she thought. I'm sure Lisa and I weren't as childish as that three years ago.

Thinking of her best friend reminded her yet again of the injustice she was nursing. She stood up and flung the last piece of cake into the water, sending the fish darting for cover. As she climbed back onto the deck her father came up from the saloon. He was whistling, his face wore a cheerful grin — which altered when he saw his daughter's scowl. "Your mother needs a hand with the dinner," he said.

Julie's scowl deepened. "I'm not hungry. Why can't Anna or Michelle help her? They're both sitting around doing nothing."

"Because it's your turn. We made a roster — remember?"

"So? I still don't see why I should have to cook if I'm not going to eat."

"Just do as you're told, young lady!" John Dykstra's voice snapped with exasperation. "I've had enough of your sulks and tantrums. I've been looking forward to this holiday for a long time — we all have — and if you think you are going to spoil it for us with your childish behaviour you are very much mistaken."

"Well, you shouldn't have brought me. I didn't want to come on your crummy old boat in the first place."

As soon as the words were out Julie regretted them. She saw the hurt in her father's eyes and remembered the years of work he had put into *Salamander* and his pride when they had finally launched her two months ago. For a moment she almost wavered but then her injured pride took possession of her again. "You told me I could stay at Lisa's," she said mutinously.

Her father looked at her hard. "Yes, and you know very well why I changed my mind. Until you show us that you can be trusted again you won't be going anywhere — especially not with Lisa. Neither one of you seems to have the slightest sense of remorse for what you did."

Julie glowered at him. Why must he make such a big deal of it? It had only been a bit of a giggle. Five-finger discounting — all the kids did it. She and Lisa had just been unlucky to get caught. And that stupid old fogey on the children's panel had been just as bad. "Stealing is stealing, young lady," he'd said pompously, "whatever your friends choose to call it. And thieves go to prison. You are being given another chance because it's your first offence and your father assures me you are sorry and have already been punished, but remember this: you cannot come before this panel a second time. If you offend again you will have to face the Children's Court and they may not deal so leniently with you."

Sanctimonious old fool! And her father had believed every word he said and grounded her for two whole months. Even worse, he had told her she would have to come away with them at Christmas instead of staying at Lisa's place. So now Lisa would be going to Atlantis and Adventure World, and meeting the boys outside Hungry Jack's, and doing all the things they had planned to do together, while she was stuck on a grotty old yacht in the stupid Abrolhos Islands with a family who didn't give a stuff about her. She felt the hot tears rush to her eyes.

"You hate me, don't you?" she cried. "You just want me to be miserable. All you care about are Paul and Anna. They can do whatever they like, but I'm never allowed to do anything. I wish they *had* put me in a home! At least there I might have got some consideration for *my* feelings — and perhaps a bit of love, too."

Her father sighed. "Of course we don't hate you, Julianna, but sometimes you make it very hard for us to like you. If you are going to sulk then perhaps you had better stay up here and I will help your mother with dinner. You can come down when you've decided to be sociable again." He turned, but then looked back. "And while you're sitting there feeling sorry for yourself, there is an old saying you might do well to think about: *'If you would be loved then first you must love and be lovable'*. It's not a one way street, you know."

As he went back down the stairs, Julie scowled after his receding back. She swore, in English and then in Dutch, but not loud enough for him to hear. It made her feel better. Her parents had insisted their children should grow up bilingual but they would have been horrified to think she knew words like that.

She leaned over the stern rail and stared out across the water. It was a beautiful evening, the first windless day they had had. The yacht was barely moving against the jetty, the sea was a huge, dappled lake and the noise of the surf no more than a whisper over Morning Reef. The sun was setting, flushing the coral shores of Long Island to a delicate pink, and in the distance the soft silhouette of the Wallabis was fading into the twilight. There was a timelessness about the Abrolhos, and a tranquility that was almost irresistible, but Julie refused to acknowledge it. Her frustrated mind saw only bland

6

dreariness. If she stayed here much longer, she thought, she would die of boredom. If only another boat would come. If only it would rain, or a storm would blow up. If only something would *happen*.

He drifted ashore eight days after the wreck, clinging to a broken mast, the last man off the dying ship. The survivors greeted him thankfully, for he was the highest authority left since Pelsaert and the skipper had sailed off in the yawl and deserted them. Here at last, they rejoiced, was somebody to take charge of them, to organise the food and water rations, to protect the women from the growing boldness of some of the crew, and to deal with the terrifying rumours that were already starting to spread. Like eager children they showed him the barrels of food and water they had rescued, their tents manufactured from pieces of sail, and their hastily improvised fish nets, bird traps, tools and cooking implements. And they brought to him for safekeeping the company's chests, crammed with jewels and fine woollen cloth and a fortune in silver Rijks dollars.

Jeronimus Cornelisz accepted their offerings and praised them for their industry. He gazed across the bleak, wind-swept atoll where terns wheeled in the sky and coral flags lay bleached as bones beneath the sun. He smiled, promising them that he would be their leader, that he would take care of them until Pelsaert, the Commandeur, came back with help. When he had reassured them he retired to the tent which they provided, and, assisted by some of the cadets and young Dutch East India Company clerks, sat down to assess the situation.

"Someone has talked," said David Zevanck. "That drunken blabbermouth Ryckert Woutersz."

Cornelisz swore. *"What did he say? Did he name any names?"*

"Only the skipper's. He was crying into his drink and complaining that Jacobsz had deserted him. He kept asking was it fair that he should be abandoned like this when he had risked his life for the skipper and slept several nights with a sword beneath his pillow, only awaiting his signal for mutiny."

"Damn!" said Cornelisz. *"He actually mentioned the word 'mutiny'?"*

"Several times," confirmed Coenraat van Huyssen.

Cornelisz thought hard. *"Something will have to be done about him,"* he said at last.

Zevanck and van Huyssen looked at each other. *"It already has,"* volunteered Zevanck. *"He . . . ah . . . disappeared last night."*

"Disappeared? How?"

The young men exchanged glances again and smiled. *"Who can tell? He was very drunk and it was a dark night. I expect he stumbled into the water and was carried away by the tide."*

"I see. Has it caused much talk?"

Van Huyssen shrugged his shoulders. *"A little, but nothing we can't deal with."*

"Good. You acted wisely," Cornelisz told them. *"But we must proceed with caution. How many can we trust?"*

The little group went into conference again. *"Twenty, perhaps,"* said Mattijs Beer, one of the ship's company of soldiers. *"But I daresay there are more who could be persuaded."*

They all looked hopefully at Cornelisz. *"You have some plan,* Mijnheer?*"*

The merchant chuckled. *"Indeed I have,"* he assured

them. "We may have lost our own ship but we still have the treasure, and sooner or later the Company is bound to send someone to look for us, whether Pelsaert and Jacobsz reach Java or not."

Seated around the makeshift table in their small, sailcloth tent, they listened in fascination while Cornelisz informed them of his intentions. His cronies grinned at one another, and Coenraat van Huyssen laughed like an excited child. "Divide and conquer," he said. "It's perfect; and if we say it is the Commandeur's orders they'll go wherever we tell them as meekly as lambs to the slaughter. Once we've got them split up among the islands in small groups we can deal with them at our leisure."

"And when the rescue ship comes... !" said Zevanck, and they all cheered.

Only Mattijs Beer still looked thoughtful. "That's all very well as far as the civilians go," he warned, "but you won't find the soldiers quite so gullible. They know something is going on. Jacop Pietersz will join us and Wouter Loos maybe, and one or two of the others, but that redheaded bastard, Weibbe Hayes, won't have any truck with us — and most of the men will follow him."

Jeronimus smiled. He pulled aside the flap of the tent and stood for a moment gazing out into the fading light, across the water to the long, low profile of Seal Island and beyond it to the small hummocks of the atolls they called the High Islands. "Don't you worry about Weibbe Hayes," he said quietly. "I have already made plans for him."

A flock of birds rose in a cloud above Long Island. Agitated, but unwilling to venture too far from their nests, they dipped and hovered above the stunted bushes like gnats over a pool. Julie wondered what could have disturbed them. She fetched the binoculars from the cockpit and, propping herself against the stern-rail, swept the island slowly from end to end. It was a strange place, long and narrow, rising like a spine out of the water. The shoreline, which at a distance appeared to be fine, white sand, revealed itself through the glasses as coral — dead, plate coral, dry as clinkers and bleached as ancient bones. It was everywhere in the Abrolhos, a fitting symbol of the bleakness and isolation of the place. Further up from the water's edge there was vegetation — tough sand-dune scrub and gaunt, under-nourished bushes.

She lifted the glasses to scan the ridge of the island's spine. At one point a marker post rose starkly against the skyline. There was something eerie about it, etched in silhouette against the darkening sky. It reminded Julie of a gallows. What a place to come for a holiday! she thought. She swung the glasses past it, travelling north-wards, but then checked and brought them back again slowly. Was that something moving in the bushes? Patiently she searched the gathering shadows. Nothing; it must have been her imagination. Yet she could have sworn... and something had disturbed the birds. Suddenly she stiffened. There it was again — a little to the north of the marker. She adjusted the focus on the binoculars and squinted through them in astonishment and disbelief. There was something there — or, more exactly, *someone.* Peering out of the bushes of that supposedly uninhabited island was, quite unmistakably, a human face.

2

IT WAS a young face, sharp and wary as a feral cat and surrounded by a thatch of shaggy, fair hair; but whether its owner was male or female it was impossible to tell in the fading light. Nor was it possible to see what he or she might be wearing. None of the figure was visible, just the head peering out from the bushes and one hand holding the foliage away from the face. The face itself was averted slightly, observing Beacon Island rather than the yacht, and there was something about the whole set-up that made Julie feel oddly uncomfortable. Why on earth would anyone want to hide on Long Island — for whoever it was obviously did not wish to be seen — and where could such a person have come from?

She swung round to the hatchway. "Dad! Come quick. There's someone here."

The whole family erupted from the saloon. "Where? Who is it? Is it a boat?" They crowded the rail of the afterdeck, trying to see for themselves.

She pointed. "Over there, on the island. There's someone hiding there."

"Show me." Paul took the glasses off her and scanned the island. "Are you sure Julie? I don't see anyone."

"Of course I'm sure. There — to the right of that marker post."

He looked again. "I still can't see anything."

"Oh, you must. Here, give them to me." She snatched the binoculars back . . . but the face had gone. Frantically, she swept the island from end to end. "It was there, I tell you. I saw it."

Paul laughed. "You're imagining things, sis. It must have been a bird."

"It wasn't. I tell you, I saw someone, as plain as daylight."

"Perhaps it was a monster," said Anna. She punched her cousin on the arm. "The Abrolhos Ness monster." And they went off into fits of giggles.

Julie rounded on them furiously. "You think you're so funny, don't you? You're pathetic, the pair of you."

"That will do, Julianna," said her mother.

"That's right, pick on me! Why don't you tell *them* to shut up for a change?"

"Julie!"

"You don't believe me, do you? You think I'm telling lies."

"Nobody thinks you're telling lies," said her father. "If you say you saw someone then I'm sure you did, or genuinely thought you did. I'll tell you what *kindje*, I'll take you over there in the dinghy first thing in the morning and we'll have a look."

"I want to go *now*. It may be too late in the morning."

John Dykstra shook his head. "No, it's getting dark. We wouldn't be able to see anything. We'll go in the morning."

"But suppose it's somebody in trouble?"

"If it was anyone in trouble he'd be on the shore, trying to attract our attention. He'd have spotted the boat quite clearly from the beach — but you said, whoever it was, was hiding in the bushes."

"Why on earth would anyone want to hide in the bushes?" asked Paul. He thought about it for a moment, then laughed. "I know; it's the Fisheries Department, spying on us to see if we've got any crayfish on board."

They all laughed — even Julie. She glanced back at the darkening shadow of Long Island. Had she imagined it? Surely she must have. There was nothing on Long Island, not even fishermen's huts, and no other boats anywhere in sight. How could there possibly be anyone there? "All right, Dad, we'll go in the morning," she said.

Her father put an arm round her shoulders and gave her an affectionate hug. "*Goede Meisje*. Good Girl. As soon as we've had breakfast we'll go and search the whole island from top to bottom. Now, tell me what it looked like, this face of yours."

Julie tried to recall it, but already the features had blurred to an abstract impression in her mind. Pale, thin, probably young; what had there been about it that had disturbed her so much? And then she remembered. "It looked . . . frightened," she said.

Weibbe Hayes, on his knees before the hole in the rock, raised cupped hands to his lips and drank. Water dripped off his beard and trickled between his fingers to fall in dark splashes onto the dusty limestone. Around him in a silent circle his soldiers waited. Their eyes followed the passage of hands to mouth, observing the movement of his throat as he swallowed. They watched him, but said nothing. At last his hands were empty. He lowered them and looked up into the ring of faces. His bluff, honest features creased into an enormous grin. "It's sweet," he said. "Sweet as milk. We've found fresh water!"

The soldiers cheered, their relief spilling over into frenzied celebration. They slapped one another on the back, cavorted about in crazy dances, scooped up handfuls of the precious liquid and flung it at one another like children at the seaside. They thrust their faces into it and gulped it down in great satisfying draughts. Water! Pure, clean, sweet-tasting rainwater! Enough to last them for months.

"Get a fire going," ordered Hayes. "We must let the others know." He glanced triumphantly around the island. "We could easily accommodate everyone here. It's big enough, there's plenty of food available and it would save carting water."

"And those little hopping creatures make a pleasant change from fish and seal meat," added Jan Carstensz, "though I'll wager when Anneken sees them she'll want to keep them all as pets!" He smiled at the thought of his plump, soft-hearted little wife trying to dissuade the castaways from their lawful prey.

On a flat limestone plateau of the western High Island they lit their brushwood fire, the prearranged announcement of their success. As the smoke curled up into the sky they settled themselves around it, weary and footsore, but triumphantly contented. They ate the last of the rations they had brought with them, toasted one another with flasks of their precious water and awaited, with eager anticipation, the arrival of the yawl which would carry

14

them back to a heroes' welcome on Batavia's Graveyard.

Through his spyglass, Jeronimus Cornelisz watched the smoke rising above High Island. He sent for Mattijs Beer. "Well?" he demanded, thrusting the glass into his hands. Beer stared in disbelief. "It's impossible. We searched both those islands thoroughly. He must be bluffing."

"Not Hayes," said Cornelisz savagely. "He wouldn't have the gumption! If he says he's found water then he's found it."

Mattijs Beer fidgeted uncomfortably. "I'm sorry, Mijnheer, but we really did search. I could have sworn..."

"You could have sworn! What bloody use is that? 'Let him search till he drops', you said. 'He'll find nothing on the High Islands'. Damn it, man, I wanted him dead — not living like a king on the only island in the whole group with fresh water."

"I'm sorry," said Beer again. He thought for a moment. "But he has no weapons — none of them have. And they can't go anywhere. We can still finish them off any time we want."

Cornelisz glowered at the young man but then, realising the truth of what he said, slowly relented. "Ja, Mattijs," he agreed, "maybe we can at that." He smiled thoughtfully. "But not just yet. There is work to be done here first."

They dropped Paul off on the southern tip of the island and Uncle Ken at the northern end. Julie and her father started at the marker and worked their way northward to meet him. John Dykstra was in his usual good humour. He crunched across the coral with purposeful strides, chatting as he went, but Julie plodded beside him in silence. In the bright light of morning it seemed ridiculous to imagine they would find anyone on the island and she felt almost foolish for having made such a fuss the night before. Almost — but not quite. Try as she might, she could not entirely banish from her mind the memory of that thin, frightened face peering out of the bushes. She glanced sideways at her father. "You think I'm making it up, don't you?"

He smiled patiently. "Have I said that?"

"You don't have to. I know what you're all thinking. I heard Aunt Jane talking to Mum last night."

"And what did she say?"

"She said I was just doing it to get attention."

Her father laughed. "Ah, Julie *kindje*, you know what Janey's like. She means well, but she has no imagination. Don't let it bother you."

"I don't," said Julie disdainfully. She looked at him sharply. "Is that what you think it was, imagination?" He made no reply so she added: "You don't believe we're going to find anything, do you?"

"Do you?" he asked gently.

She didn't want to answer that, but in the end she shook her head. "No," she confessed, "not now. It seems sort of . . . I don't know . . . But I did see someone, Dad, I know I did, as plain as I see you."

He patted her on the shoulder. "Well, let's have a good look, shall we? And don't worry about it. If we find anything, that's fine; if not, well, it's a lovely day for beachcombing, and we need the exercise anyway."

It was a good hour later when they all met back at the

dinghy to compare notes and by then they had searched every part of the island. Uncle Ken had found a glass fishing float washed up on the beach and Paul was carrying an enormous green bottle — but of Julie's mysterious stranger, or any clues to his existence, there was no trace. She waited fiercely for one of them to start teasing her but they were all too engrossed with their trophies. Paul was already considering how to turn his into a lamp while Uncle Ken had decided the float, still in its rope net, would make an ideal decoration for his bar. They were loading them into the boat when Paul suddenly pointed and said excitedly: "Hey, look, we've got visitors."

They all looked over at *Salamander* and saw another vessel — a fishing boat — tied up behind her. John Dykstra grinned delightedly. "Bran muffins for morning tea," he predicted. "Your mother won't miss the opportunity to do some entertaining." And sure enough, as they tied up to the duckboard of *Salamander*, the aroma of baking cakes wafted out from the galley to greet them.

The visitors — two fishermen — were already ensconced in the saloon, with mugs of coffee in their hands. They introduced themselves and Ian, the skipper, complimented John Dykstra on his boat. He confessed that it was his dream to build a yacht some day and sail off into the sunset. Julie couldn't imagine anything worse than spending the rest of her life on a yacht, and said so quite bluntly. Her mother frowned at her, shaking her head in her best 'That will do, Julianna' manner, but Ian only smiled and said, "Ah, well, horses for courses. We're all a bit mad in this game."

Julie decided she liked him. He was a slight, dark,

softly-spoken man, quiet almost to the point of shyness. It was his partner, Graham, who did most of the talking. Graham was an extrovert — big, friendly, loud of voice and never at a loss for words. He tucked into Mrs Dykstra's bran muffins with great gusto and regaled his hosts with vivid tales of their fishing adventures. Anna told him all about 'the great Long Island manhunt', as she called it, and he roared with laughter. Julie could have died from embarrassment. She blushed furiously, planning a hundred unpleasant fates for her sister next time she got her alone, and tried to kick her under the table, but Anna had her feet well out of reach. It was Ian who saved the day. When all the mirth had died down he said quietly: "You may laugh, but she wouldn't be the first person to see ghosts out here in the Abrolhos."

"Hey," said Julie, "I never claimed it was a ghost."

He smiled at her. "Don't you believe in ghosts?"

"Of course not . . . I mean . . . I don't know. I've never really thought about it. Do you?"

"Oh, no," he said. "Back in Geraldton, safe and snug in my little suburban house, I'd laugh my head off at the very mention of the word, but out here . . . well, it's different somehow, and goodness knows there's been enough blood spilt on these islands to spawn a multitude of ghosts."

"Blood?" asked Paul. "Why? What happened?" He turned to his father. "I bet it has something to do with those anchors and cannon we dived on yesterday."

"Has it?" Julie asked Ian. "They came off a ship called the *Batavia*, didn't they? She's marked on our chart. Do you know what happened to her?"

Ian nodded. "She was a Dutch East Indiaman — the pride of the fleet — on her first voyage from Holland to

Batavia — what we now call Djakarta — back in 1629. She ran aground on Morning Reef."

"Were there any survivors?"

"Oh yes, over two hundred. They came ashore here on Beacon Island. They called it 'The Island of *Batavia*'s Graveyard'. Their commander, Francisco Pelsaert, with the ship's skipper and about forty of the crew, sailed off in an open boat to look for water. When they found none, his sailors insisted they should make for Java to get help, so they went off and left the others to their fate. The castaways were very bitter and the island Pelsaert sailed from — the larger of those two little islands between here and the reef — they named Traitors Island."

"But what about the blood?" asked Paul. "You said there was blood spilt. Were they fighting for places in the boat?"

"No," said Ian. "Pelsaert and his crew left secretly, at night. No-one realised they had gone till the next morning. For those left behind, things were very bad at first. The water ran out and it looked as if they would all die of thirst; several of them did. But then it rained, and the survivors were able to collect enough water in barrels to keep them going and, of course, there was plenty of food: fish, seals, birds' eggs. They made tents out of *Batavia*'s sails, and small boats out of timber from the wreck. They salvaged barrels and chests that floated ashore after the ship broke up. They could have gone on living like that for months."

"So what happened to them?"

Ian looked round the group of curious, expectant faces. "Murder," he said. "Cold-blooded murder."

The clumsy bundle of driftwood bumped and scraped across the shallows, aided by the current and the prevailing wind. When the water was no longer deep enough to carry it forward the men clinging to it abandoned it and, dragging themselves to their feet, began to stumble towards the shore. There were four of them; weak, ragged ad exhausted; they had been in the water for hours. The jagged coral grazed their legs and cut their feet to ribbons but they staggered on, too weary even to curse. When they reached the shore they collapsed on the narrow strip of sand and lay like men already dead. It was here that Weibbe Hayes and his men found them. The soldiers carried them back to the shelter they had built, gave them food and water, bound their bleeding feet with strips of cloth and dried out their sodden clothing. Only then did Hayes begin to question them.

Cornelis Jansz, the young clerk, shivering in his borrowed coat and still bleeding from a cutlass wound, acted as their spokesman. As he sobbed out his incoherent tale the soldiers stared at one another in horror. They had suspected treachery but this was beyond all imagining.

"We watched the boat come ashore," said Cornelis, his eyes dark with remembered terror. "Some of us even went to meet them. We'd seen what happened on Traitors Island but we didn't understand . . . we thought . . ." He put his head in his hands and began to weep brokenly.

"It's all right lad," said Hayes gently. "Take your time and tell us exactly what happened."

"They were like dogs," sobbed the boy. "Like a pack of starving wolves. And we had nothing to fight with. They made a game of it, three or four of them slashing at one victim and arguing over who had struck the death blow. Even the children — even the little cabin boys — they killed. I saw . . . ach, Gott." He buried his face in his

hands again and rocked to and fro, keening softly.

"Goede Hemel!" said Hayes. "How many of you were living on Seals Island? Did they leave anyone alive?"

"They spared the women, I think," said one of the others. "And some of the younger boys; a handful maybe, I don't know."

"How did you manage to escape?"

"We were lucky. A few of us had been planning for some time to try and get to the High Islands and we'd collected driftwood to make a raft. When we saw what was happening, four of us made a run for it. They chased us into the water but once we were out of the shallows they were afraid to follow us."

"Who were they?" asked Hayes grimly.

The survivors looked at one another, remembering. "Zevank, van Huyssen, Hans Jacobs, Cornelisz Pietersz: about half a dozen I suppose," said one of them. "But he was not with them. He stayed behind and watched while they did his dirty work."

"He? You mean Jeronimus Cornelisz?"

The man nodded and spat savagely on the ground. "Ja, may he rot in hell; he was the one who gave the orders."

"So," said Hayes. "Now we know why he never sent a boat for us. He never intended us to find water on this island — he sent us here to die!" He threw back his head and laughed. "Well, the joke is on you Jeronimus Cornelisz. Here we are alive and well, and with all the food and water we could possibly need. All we have to do is keep ourselves that way until help arrives and, by God, we'll yet watch you swing from the gallows at Batavia castle."

There was a silence; then Jan Carstensz said bitterly: "And do you imagine the same thought has not occurred to him? How long do you think it will be before he decides to do something about it?"

21

Nobody answered him. They stared out across the water in the direction of Batavia's Graveyard, *thinking longingly of the guns and pikes they had left behind in Cornelisz's hands — and wondering how long they had to prepare their defences.*

3

THAT NIGHT they had a barbecue on Beacon Island. Julie and Paul made hamburger patties while the others went fishing in the dinghy and returned with several grilling-sized snapper. Ian and Graham produced some steak, which they very generously shared. Paul drooled at the mouth when he saw it, and his family teased him unmercifully. They kept very little meat on the boat, preferring to live on the fish they caught, but Paul was a self-confessed carnivore and declared himself ready to kill for a juicy steak.

Ian and Graham had appointed themselves hosts for the evening. They commandeered a barbecue from one of the huts and had the embers glowing nicely by the time the Dykstras arrived. It seemed strange to be sitting in the front garden of unknown crayfishermen, cooking steak on their hotplate. Julie felt as though someone might come along at any minute and demand to know what they were doing there. She kept glancing over her shoulder, even though Graham assured her nobody ever minded, as long as they did no damage.

Whatever the absent owners might have had to say about their presence, the other inhabitants certainly objected. Every patch of scrub and wisp of ground cover appeared to house a nesting tern; little, brown, puffball chicks scurried about in the bushes, piping at the intruders in small anxious voices. The mother birds spread angry wings and arched their necks and chattered like badly-tuned sewing machines. Julie couldn't blame them; after all, these islands had been their home for centuries, long before Europeans discovered them.

There was a nest with an egg in it under the garden wall, quite close to the barbecue. The parent birds had flown off when the humans invaded their territory, and now they hovered nearby, squawking angrily, sometimes even landing on the wall, but not quite brave enough to return to their nest. Julie felt very guilty; suppose the egg became too cold and failed to hatch? She wanted to point it out to the others, but she doubted if they'd care. After all, what was one egg more or less on an island smothered with the things? They'd probably laugh at her, like they always did, and she didn't fancy being made fun of in front of strangers. She munched on her steak and tried to put it from her mind.

"Ah, this is the life," said John Dykstra, stretching out in his deckchair and taking a long pull on his can of beer. "I wonder how much longer this weather can last? I've never known it so calm."

"Make the most of it," advised Graham. "It could be blowing a gale by tomorrow. You can never tell in the Abrolhos."

After they'd finished eating, Paul began to strum his guitar and, when Graham produced a mouth-organ, a lively sing-along soon developed. Julie was not in the mood for jollity. She wandered off by herself, picking her way quite easily in the moonlight, down past the huts and out to the thin strip of beach, where small waves lapped against the sand and the fishermen's jetties reached blackly across the shallow water like the arms of an octopus. In the water near one of them, only about a metre down, a cannon off the wrecked *Batavia* lay on the seabed. Julie had seen it before. It had been put there by one of the crayfishermen and a notice on the jetty directed attention to its watery showcase. She walked out along the wooden planks and stood peering down at it but, even in the moonlight, it was too dark to make out its shape through the ripples.

She lifted her eyes and looked out across the water to Traitors Island. Beyond it she could just make out the thin cream of surf over Morning Reef. She remembered the story Ian had told them and it didn't take much imagination to picture the dark form of a ship, crippled and helpless on the jagged coral, or to hear the screams of her terrified passengers. She could imagine the panic and the struggle for the boats; the hysteria of those who could not swim; the children clinging to their mothers in bewildered terror: and all around them a cold, foaming cauldron of white water and the implacable roar of the reef. Here, on this beach behind her, the survivors must finally have staggered ashore, cold, exhausted, thankful beyond expression, praising God for their deliverance. If they had only known ... She shivered, suddenly cold despite the warmth of the evening, and, turning, made her way back to the barbecue and the cheerful companionship of her family.

It was nearly midnight before the party broke up. As they walked back along the jetty to their boats the wind

— that inexorable Abrolhos southerly — was starting to rise again and they guessed that by morning the weather would be back to normal. Already there were little white-topped ripples scudding across the channel between Beacon and Long Islands.

"We might go across to the Wallabis tomorrow," suggested John Dykstra. "If this wind keeps up it would be a good run."

"Good idea," said Ian. "We plan to leave first thing in the morning and will probably anchor in Turtle Bay tomorrow night, so we might see you there. But, in case we don't, have a good holiday — and maybe we'll catch you some other time. Once you've been in the Abrolhos you always come back again, eventually. We'll try not to make too much noise going out," he added with a grin.

They all shook hands and then retired sleepily to their respective boats. On board *Salamander* Aunt Jane offered to make coffee, but there were no takers. Within half an hour the lights were out and the yacht was in silence. Only Julie lay awake, unable to sleep. Her thoughts were still on Perth and her friend Lisa and all the things she would rather be doing. So they were going to the Wallabis tomorrow... big deal! Once you've seen one of these crummy islands you've seen the lot, she thought. What was so exciting about a few wallabies, that you could see in any old wildlife park, and a couple of ancient wells? She would much rather have gone fishing with Ian and Graham. At least they would be doing something useful.

Thinking about the two fishermen, she suddenly remembered something Graham had said about catching sharks round the jetty here at night. It would be fun to catch a shark; she had never seen a live one close up.

Once or twice she had hooked them while fishing for snapper from the dinghy, but they had always managed to break the line and escape before she got them close enough to the surface to take a look at them. Impulsively she jumped out of bed and pulled on some old clothes, not forgetting a pair of sturdy sneakers — she had seen Paul once get a hook stuck in his bare foot during a moonlight fishing expedition. Carefully, so as not to wake the others, she rummaged in the freezer for some suitable bait; then, on tiptoe, she crept up to the deck.

The trawl lines clamped to the side rails of the boat were rigged with lures for catching tuna, but it was the work of a moment to unfasten one of them and attach in its place a steel trace and big shark hook. The hardest part was getting the solid-frozen bait onto the hook. Julie cursed and struggled but at last the big chunk of bonito was firmly impaled. She tossed it over the side and watched it fall with a loud plop into the water. A few bubbles rose and broke on the surface as it disappeared. She tightened the drag and settled down to wait. Now that she was out of bed she suddenly began to feel sleepy and for a while she debated whether to go back to her bunk and leave the line set till morning. In the end she decided to stay. It was peaceful out on the deck and, besides, if she caught anything she didn't want anyone else pulling it in and claiming ownership.

The birds were still restless over Long Island. They wheeled like ghosts in the moonlight and their cries echoed thinly across the water. She watched them through half-closed eyes, delighting in the untaught grace of their movements. What it must be to possess such freedom! And yet they were totally unaware of it. No-one had ever told them how lucky they were.

Feeling a little sorry for herself, she stood up and gave a tug on the line, just to encourage anything that might be lurking down there. Suddenly she stiffened, staring in the direction of Long Island; the line slipped, forgotten, through her fingers. From somewhere near the middle of the island, close to where she had seen the face yesterday morning, a thin ribbon of smoke curled up into the sky.

She stared at it in half-fearful excitement. So she had been right after all, there *was* someone on the island! But who could it be and how could they have missed him when they searched the island yesterday? She was on the point of calling out to the others when she checked herself and thought better of it. No, it would be useless telling any of them. They would invent all sorts of uninteresting reasons for smoke or even say it wasn't smoke at all, and, even if she managed to convince them, Dad would never agree to take the dinghy over there tonight. He would insist on waiting till morning and by then whoever it was would have vanished again. If she wanted to solve this mystery she would have to do it herself. They'll laugh on the other side of their faces, she thought fiercely, when I come back with proof.

The big problem was to get the dinghy away without anyone hearing her. She dared not risk starting the motor. Turning a questing face to the wind, she discovered it was blowing, quite strongly now, from the southeast. She dropped a piece of paper into the water and watched it carefully as it floated away in the moonlight. Perfect, she decided; as long as she kept the head of the dinghy pointing well to port, the wind and current should carry her ashore on Long Island just about where she wanted. She would hardly need to row.

And coming back there would be no need for secrecy — she could make as much noise as she liked.

Half in awe at her own daring, she climbed down onto the duckboard. In the dinghy she untied the oars and slipped them silently into the rowlocks; then she cast off the mooring line and, with a final shove, pushed herself away from *Salamander*. She was on her own. The boat rocked gently in the water; little waves slapped against the sides; the night air smelled of seaweed and salt water. A sharp wind fanned her cheek, blowing her hair into a damp tangle, and she turned up the collar of her sweater, snuggling thankfully into its thick warmth. The current was running strongly and she was delighted with the accuracy of her calculations. By using the starboard oar as a rudder, and paddling from time to time to hold her course, she was able to steer almost due west and let it carry her across the channel. It would be a wet, bumpy ride back but she was too excited to worry about that.

At last the bottom of the boat began to scrape on the coral — time to get out and push. She rolled up the legs of her jeans and hunted around for the torch which was always kept in the dinghy with the fishing gear. It wasn't there. Paul must have taken it when he cleaned up after their fishing trip. She cursed her brother for his excessive efficiency and herself for not thinking to check before leaving. Even with the help of a full moon it would be difficult to search the island without it. For a moment she considered going back, but her stubbornness got the better of her. She had come this far, she would carry on. At least she could make sure there was no boat anchored on the far side of the island and if the worst came to the worst she could wait till dawn to explore further.

She slid over the side, shivering a little as the cold water lapped around her knees, and set off for the shore. Getting through the shallows proved harder than she had anticipated. The water was deeper than she had expected, the bottom treacherous, and without the torch it was impossible to see where she was going. Stumbling and cursing, stubbing her toes and scraping her shins, pushing and pulling till her arms ached with exhaustion, she dragged the dinghy around and across the protruding lumps of coral until at last she reached the shore. She hauled the dinghy as far up the beach as she could manage and, carrying the anchor well beyond the tide line, buried it securely. Then she flung herself down on the coral, panting like a spent puppy, too weary to take another step.

She must have dozed off, for she woke some time later, cold and panic-stricken, trying to remember where she was and what she was doing there. She sat up and looked back across the water to Beacon Island. It was so dark she could make out neither the jetty nor the boats tied up to it. She shivered, her sense of adventure suddenly beginning to evaporate. What ever had possessed her to embark on such a ridiculous enterprise? If there really was someone on the island, he quite plainly didn't want to be found — and here she was preparing to spy on him, quite alone, and about as agile in the darkness as a runaway rhinoceros. She must have been mad, even to think of it. And surely it hadn't been this dark when she set out; what had happened to the moon? She scrambled to her feet and looked upwards. Above her a sliver of light, no thicker than the rind on a slice of melon, glowed palely against the dark sky. She stared at it in disbelief. It couldn't be: there was a full moon tonight; she'd seen it. Suddenly she was swept with terror, something was happening here — something weird and terrible, beyond her comprehension — and her only thought now was to get down to the dinghy and back to the safety and security of *Salamander*.

She ran down the beach, her shoes squelching and clattering on the dead coral, but when she reached the spot where she thought she had left her boat it was nowhere to be seen. Frantically she searched up and down the shoreline: nothing. It had vanished, totally and silently, without a mark or scrape or furrow in the shingle to show that it had ever been there.

Her heart seemed to freeze inside her chest. There was no way that boat could have drifted off on its own. Someone must have taken it. But how? And why? And where were the marks where she had dragged it up the beach? And why had the moon suddenly changed?

An eclipse, she comforted herself. It must be a lunar eclipse. Yet it did not look like one, even to her untrained eye. She was on the verge of hysteria, but somehow she made herself think calmly. If someone had stolen the dinghy then it could only be the person who was hiding on the island; and if he had gone then she was safe, at least for tonight. And tomorrow morning her parents would miss her and come looking for her. If they discovered her absence before the fishermen left they could borrow their dinghy; otherwise one of the men would have to swim over and bring her diving gear. It would be a long swim back against the current, even with flippers; Paul would be furious if they made him do it. She giggled, thinking about it, and suddenly felt much braver. Well, since she was stuck here she might as well do what she had come for in the first place

31

and explore the island. She glanced up towards the ridge, trying to get her bearings, but in the darkness she could no longer see the marker. She had been almost directly beneath it when she landed, so if she walked straight up the slope she should finish up just about where she had seen the smoke.

Quite cheerful now, she left the beach and plodded up through the scrub, scattering indignant birds as she went. They screeched and swore at her, hovering just above her head, and, as soon as she had passed, swooped back to settle on their nests. She could hear nestlings in the bushes, too, and hoped fervently she wasn't treading on them. At last she came to the place she was looking for. It was a sandy basin hollowed into the slope of the ridge. The sides rose quite steeply, covered with creepers and small bushes that sprouted a spongy, succulent-type foliage, something like the branches of a frangipani. Around the lower rim were clumps of reeds and, in the centre, surrounded by a flat, sandy shore, was a shallow salt lake. She had seen it yesterday morning and marked it then as a likely hiding place. Now she was certain it was where the smoke had come from. Cautiously she dropped to her knees and crawled forward to peer over the lip.

The hairs on the back of her neck prickled with excitement. On the northern shore of the little lake somebody had raised a tent and beside it was the remains of a campfire. It was nearly dead but a few embers still glowed among the ashes and, over them, a pot with a ladle in it hung suspended from a tripod. Steam from this pot, together with a stray wisp of smoke, rose and dissipated in the breeze. Julie stared at it. Here at last was proof of her mysterious stranger —

but what could he be doing here and why had he stolen her boat? As she was pondering these questions the front of the tent suddenly twitched open and a face looked out. It peered up the slope to where she was crouching and she jerked backwards in shock. Oh, God, he was still there! But who had taken the dinghy? Could there be two of them?

At that moment she heard the scrunch of footsteps behind her. She scrambled to her feet but before she could run someone pushed her violently in the back. She fell sprawling into the scrub. A knee ground into her back. A hand seized her hair and pulled her head back so hard she thought her neck would break. Something cold and sharp jabbed against her throat and a voice hissed in her ear: "Make one sound and I'll kill you."

Somewhere through the chaos of her terrified mind it registered that the words had been spoken in Dutch.

4

JULIE could not have cried out, even had she
dared. The pressure on her windpipe was so great it
was all she could do to breathe. She lay weakly where
she had fallen and when her captor realised she was not
going to struggle he very slowly relaxed his grip on her
hair. Her head dropped forward again and she sucked
air back into her lungs in grateful gulps. After a moment
the knife was removed from her throat. The voice said:
"Get up." At the same time a hand seized her collar and
hauled her to her feet. Slipping and stumbling, her
mind a whirl of terrified confusion, she was pushed
down the slope towards the salt lake.

As they approached the camp site the flap on the little
tent was pulled aside and the face looked out at her
again. To her amazement it was quickly joined by a
second one and, after a whispered conversation, two
ragged figures crept out. They stood side by side on the
sandy shore, two boys of about her own age, eyeing her
with hostile curiosity. Her captor tightened his grip on
her collar and said with grim satisfaction: "Well, I

caught him. He was spying on us from the top of the hill!"

The boys continued to stare at her. Finally one of them said: "But it's a girl, Dirk!" and the other, a sudden flash of recognition lighting his face, exclaimed: "It's Annetje; Annetje Maertens!"

"Annetje?" The hand holding her collar dropped to her shoulder and jerked her around. She found herself looking into the features of a boy perhaps twelve months older than herself. Here at last was her mysterious fugitive. He was slightly taller than she — thin, almost gaunt, with angular, fine-boned features and enormous eyes that looked very black in the darkness. His clothes were little more than rags, and his hair, stiffened by long exposure to salt water, stuck out in spiky tufts around his face. He stared at her for a moment in bafflement and then said, "Annetje! What are you doing here? We thought you were dead."

Suddenly they were all talking at once. Flinging questions at her in rapid Dutch, which, while similar to the language she spoke at home, was different enough to fill her with confusion. Julie opened her mouth to speak, but instead burst into tears. The noise, the language, the bizarre happenings of the evening were all too much for her. She buried her head against Dirk's shoulder and sobbed hysterically. The boy put his arms round her, stroking her hair as one might a frightened puppy.

"It's all right Annetje. I'm sorry. We didn't mean to frighten you, but we didn't know who you were. We thought you were one of *them*, come to spy on us."

"We thought you were dead," said one of the others. "We hadn't seen you since the night of the wreck. We thought you'd drowned."

Julie pressed her face into Dirk's shoulder and made a small muffled sound that could have meant anything. Now that the first terror had passed, her mind had started to function again and she was beginning to feel her way cautiously. Something very strange was happening here but this Annetje, whoever she might be, apparently posed no threat to the boys and was therefore in no danger. For the time being it might not be a bad idea to assume her identity.

She lifted her face and wiped her eyes with her sleeve. "I'm not hurt," she said, in faltering Dutch. "Just a bit bruised, that's all." And she managed a rather wobbly grin.

Dirk smiled back at her. From within the security of his arms Julie turned to study the others. In the gloom of the night it was hard to make out their features. One was darker and possibly a little younger than his companion, but their faces were both etched with that sharp, feral tension that she had already observed in Dirk's. Underneath their toughness they were all quite plainly terrified of something.

"Where did you get those strange clothes?" one of them asked her.

She thought frantically, wondering what they could find so strange about a pair of jeans and a sweater. "I found them," she said, " . . . amongst the stuff that was salvaged."

She watched their faces anxiously, but Dirk laughed, misunderstanding her fear. "There's no need to feel guilty," he said, a trifle bitterly. "What is your little theft, compared to the way *he* makes free of all the chests?"

There was something in his voice that made Julie feel

decidedly uncomfortable. Who was this mysterious *he*? She longed to ask, but evidently Annetje was presumed to know all about him, so she held her tongue.

Still a little suspiciously, the dark boy asked: "Why did you come over here? Are you sure *he* did not send you?"

"No-one sent me," she said indignantly. "I saw your smoke and I was curious, so I took the boat and..."

"A boat?" It was Dirk. "You have a boat?"

"Yes, but..."

"God be praised; where is it?"

"It's gone," she said, suddenly remembering. "I left it on the beach and when I looked for it again... I thought you'd taken it."

"Gone!" said the dark boy savagely. "You stupid little fool! Do you realise what you've done? That boat would have been our one chance of escape, and you've lost it. And what do you think will happen when they discover it's missing?'

"They'll come looking for me," said Julie. "What's wrong with that?"

The boy stared at her wildly. "You've killed us," he moaned. "Oh, God, you've got us all killed." He put his head in his hands and began to wail inconsolably.

Dirk slapped him hard across the face. "Stop it, Claas; stop it. No-one's going to kill us. Pull yourself together." He waited, and gradually the wailing subsided. "That's better. Now listen to me. They won't kill us, simply because they don't know we are still alive. Think about it. If they come here they'll be looking for Annetje and the boat, not for us, and when they see the boat isn't here they'll go away again. Besides, who would expect Annetje to come here? Anyone trying to escape from *Batavia*'s Graveyard would make for Soldiers Island, not this one."

"I . . . I suppose so." Claas still sounded dubious, but at least he had stopped trembling, and his hysterical crying had ceased.

Dirk smiled at him encouragingly. "That's better. Now you and Jan go back to bed and try to get some sleep. I'll take the first watch. I want to talk to Annetje."

Julie listened to the exchange in bewilderment, struggling to understand what they were saying. What on earth was going on here: all this wild talk of soldiers and killings? And *Batavia*'s Graveyard: wasn't that the old name Ian had used for Beacon Island? Perhaps the Dutch still called it that. There were a million questions she wanted to ask. Who was Annetje? How had they all come to be wrecked here? And, most of all, who was this man of whom they were all so mortally afraid?

When the others had disappeared into the tent, Dirk led her over to the remains of the campfire. "Sit down," he said. "Would you like some soup?"

It smelled overwhelmingly fishy. She shook her head.

"Suit yourself." He lifted a ladleful from the pot and put it to his own lips. She watched him as he drank. When he had finished he wiped his mouth with the back of his hand; then, replacing the ladle, he turned at last to look at her. His eyes studied her face minutely and she waited nervously, wondering what he wanted. Suddenly he said: "Suppose now you tell me who you really are."

Panic grabbed her. She tried to scramble to her feet, but he put a hand on her arm and pulled her back. "You're not Annetje, are you?" he demanded.

A thousand explanations whirled through her mind,

but none of them seemed adequate. In the end she could only shake her head. He put a hand under her chin and lifted her face. To her great relief she saw he was smiling. "I thought not," he said. "You look like her; you'd probably fool most of the others, but I knew her better than they did." He spoke quite gently. "If you are not Annetje, then who are you and where did you come from? You weren't on the ship, were you?"

It was all too much for her. She put her hands over her face and began to cry again. "I don't know," she wept. "I don't know anything any more. It's all gone crazy. Who are you, Dirk? Where's this ship you keep talking about? What's happening to me?"

He put his arms around her again, muffling her sobs against the front of his shirt. "Hush," he soothed. "Hush, you'll wake the others. Don't be frightened; I'm not going to hurt you. Just tell me how you got here and I'll explain everything to you."

Haltingly, she told him the whole story. He heard her out in silence, but when she had finished he said: "Now it is I who am puzzled. Where is this Perth you talk of?"

She stared at him. "What do you mean, where's Perth? It's in Western Australia, of course."

"And where is Western Australia?"

He had to be joking. "Oh don't be stupid," she said. "It's over there." She waved a vague hand in the direction of the mainland.

It was his turn to stare. His eyes opened like moon-flowers. "The Southland!" He breathed the word in an awe-stricken whisper. "You came in a boat from the unknown Southland? You live there?"

"Eh?" she blinked at him; then, very slowly, the significance of what he had said began to dawn on her.

"Dirk," she said quietly. "The ship you were on — the one that was wrecked — what was her name?"

"She was the *Batavia*," said Dirk. "The *Batavia*, out of Amsterdam."

"But it's not possible," she whispered. "You're joking, aren't you? Tell me you're playing a trick on me."

"Of course I'm not joking," he said. "Do you think I don't know the name of my own ship?"

"But, Dirk, the *Batavia* sank three hundred years ago! I've seen the cannon and the anchors. I've swum down and touched them on the seabed."

He laughed. "Your brain must be addled. Do I look three hundred years old?" But somehow he didn't sound at all sure of himself.

"Then how did I get here? Where did I come from? Look at my clothes. Didn't you tell me they were strange?"

They stared at each other in mutual fear and distrust.

"You don't look like a witch," he ventured at last.

"Of course I'm not a witch!" She was nearly hysterical. "It's *you! You* shouldn't be here! You're not real, are you? You're . . . you're a ghost!"

His hand tightened round her arm till she winced. "Oh, I'm real all right," he said grimly, "and so are Jan and Claas. But if it's ghosts you want . . ." He broke off and she felt the shudder that ran through his body. "It must be *his* doing. They say *he* is in league with the devil," and he reached inside his shirt as though to clutch some talisman concealed beneath it.

"*He?*" asked Julie.

"Cornelisz!" The boy spat the name as though the very word was an obscenity. "Jeronimus Cornelisz, the undermerchant. He is an Adamite, a follower of

Torrentius. He believes neither in the devil nor in hell and boasts that he has never been baptised." He laughed, savagely. "And to think old man Bastiensz once accused *me* of being a heretic! Well, now the poor sod knows what heresy is really like — though I doubt if he'll live long enough to profit from his knowledge."

Jeronimus Cornelisz: Ian had mentioned that name. Julie wracked her brains, trying to remember what he had said about him. How she wished now that she had paid more attention to the story. "Didn't he try to steal the ship — he and the skipper?"

"*Ja*," said Dirk. "That was their plan, but Jacobsz's carelessness ruined their chances. They had it all worked out: nail down the hatches on the soldiers, murder the passengers and those of the crew who would not join them, throw the Commandeur overboard, then off to Malacca to divide the spoils and turn the *Batavia* into a pirate ship."

"So what happened?" asked Julie.

"What happened? The stupid fool ran her aground. Smashed her up on a reef during his own watch while he was busy dreaming of his doxy. So much for his precious mutiny! He's gone off to Java with Commandeur Pelsaert, in the ship's boat, to try and bring back help. I hope they hang him when he gets there."

Julie's mind was reeling. She tried to make some sense out of it all, to understand how she could have slipped back through three centuries, but all she could manage was a jumbled memory of a sleep on the beach, a vanished boat and a different moon. "I've got to get back," she said. "I've got to get back to *Salamander*."

He stared at her intently. "Oh, God," he said softly. "You really mean it, don't you? You really have come from another time."

She wasn't listening. Jumping to her feet, she began to walk back up the hill. He ran after her.

"Wait; you can't." She quickened her pace but he caught up with her and seized her by the shoulders. "Stop, Annetje — whoever you are — you can't go back. There's no way."

"There's got to be," she said, trying to shake him off.

"But your boat's gone."

"I'll swim."

"Don't be ridiculous." He clung to her tightly. "It's pitch black; you'd drown — or the sharks would get you. Besides, supposing you do reach Beacon Island, or whatever you call it. Your people aren't here. This is *now*, Annetje. There's only Cornelisz and his men."

"Stop calling me Annetje!" she shouted, lashing out in her desperation. "My name is Julie. I don't belong here and I want to go home."

"You want to go home! God in heaven; don't you imagine I want to go home? Don't you think we all do? Have you any idea what we've been through in the last five days? Grubbing around in the bushes, too frightened to show our faces, waiting for them to come back and finish us off."

"What do you mean?" she asked, shocked out of her own panic by the raw anguish in his voice. "Why are you so sure someone wants to kill you?"

He closed his eyes and ran an exhausted hand through his hair. "Sit down Julie. I'd better tell you the whole story. But I warn you, it's not very pleasant."

She listened in growing horror while he told her of what had happened since the wreck: of how Pelsaert and Jacobsz had deserted them; how Cornelisz had given himself the title of Captain General and the reign of terror that had followed his assumption of leadership. "He has a following of about twenty or so," said Dirk, "all men who were in on the mutiny plot; and there are others, as many again perhaps, who obey him out of fear. But for the rest . . . " He drew a finger across his throat in a grim gesture.

Julie shuddered. "Could no-one stop him?"

Dirk shook his head. "No-one knew until it was too late. The soldiers might have resisted, but he sent them all to the High Islands to look for water — except those few he thought he could trust. He expected them to die, for the islands had already been searched once. But they didn't. They are still alive. I have seen the smoke of their fires."

He paused for a moment, as if considering the ramifications of their survival, then continued: "After the soldiers had gone, he said some of us must go to the other islands. He said it was too crowded on *Batavia*'s Graveyard. Some forty of us were brought over here and a dozen or so made their camp on Traitors Island. About two weeks ago the people on Traitors Island built themselves a raft and tried to escape to Soldiers Island. They must have guessed what was going to happen. Jeronimus sent three of his men in a boat to intercept them. We could see it all from the beach. They threw them into the sea and those who managed to swim ashore were murdered as they struggled through the shallows to *Batavia*'s Graveyard. We could hear them screaming for help."

"Dear God," breathed Julie. A terrible thought struck her. "Dirk, the people here? You said there were forty of you."

Dirk was silent for so long she thought he was not going to answer her, but presently he drew a deep breath and said in a hard, tightly-controlled voice: "Eight days ago they came over here in a boat; half a dozen of them. They went through the island systematically. Cornelis Jansz and Marcus Symonsz escaped on a raft with the Wagenaars brothers, but the rest of the men, eighteen in all, were butchered and dragged into the sea for the sharks. Only the women and children and a handful of the boys were spared."

"But if they spared the women...?" Julie hardly dared to frame her question.

Dirk's thin body shook with suppressed emotion as he answered it. "They thought better of it. Three days later they came back to finish the job. Claas and Jan and I managed to hide in the bushes, but the others... even Mayken Soers, who was seven months pregnant..." He broke off and sat with clenched fists, staring into the darkness, reliving the nightmare of the massacre.

Julie watched him in silence, longing to offer some comfort but afraid even to touch him. How did anyone cope with that kind of terror? How could you live with it and still retain your sanity? Suddenly her own little rebellion against adult authority seemed absurdly childish.

At last Dirk spoke again. "They will come back, you know." He said it with a terrible calmness. "We cannot hide for ever. Sooner or later they will realise we are still alive and then they will come back for us."

For the first time Julie saw her own danger. She said: "Dirk, we've got to escape. We can't just sit here and wait for them to come and kill us. You said something about a raft — couldn't we build one?"

"We've started," said Dirk, "but it takes time to collect enough driftwood. There's nothing on the island to make it from." He hugged her suddenly. "Perhaps you're an omen to us, Julie. Maybe now you're here we will succeed. Maybe you were sent to bring us luck."

"I hope so," she replied. "I certainly haven't brought much to myself." Suddenly she remembered something else. "Dirk, who is this Annetje that you all mistook me for? Was she killed by the mutineers?"

Dirk shook his head slowly and something told Julie that the girl had been more to him than just a casual acquaintance. "No," he said. "She drowned trying to get ashore, soon after the wreck. And perhaps it was just as well," he added bitterly. "Hers was an easier death than most of us can expect."

Julie was silent for a moment; then she said gently: "Tell me about her, Dirk."

He hesitated, as though unwilling to drag up painful memories, but at last he confided: "She was the daughter of one of the French soldiers. Her father was also drowned in the wreck. Her mother was dead and he was taking Annetje to make a new life for them both in Batavia." He sighed; then, turning to look at Julie, suddenly smiled again, shaking his head a little. "You really are incredibly like her, you know; even your voice; she spoke terrible Dutch! Her real name was Anne-Marie but we called her Annetje because it was easier."

"You were very fond of her, weren't you?"

He nodded.

"Dirk, I have been thinking. If it would not hurt you too much it might be better if I went on pretending to be

45

Annetje. How would I ever explain the truth about myself, and where I come from, to the others?"

"The same thing had occurred to me," said Dirk. "They would be frightened of you. They might call you a witch."

"But you are not afraid?"

Dirk laughed. "Oh, I'm damned already — or so the predikant would have me believe."

"Why?"

"Because of this." He fumbled at his neck and pulled out a string of beads from underneath his shirt.

Julie looked at it closely. "It's a rosary," she said.

He seemed surprised. "You have seen one before?"

"Well, of course. Lots of people have them. I've got one myself, at home. Did Annetje give it to you?"

He nodded. "I think in your time people must be a lot more tolerant," he said thoughtfully. "Maistre Gyjsbert, the predikant, told me a rosary was a popish blasphemy and that if I wore it I would surely go to hell."

"And what did you say to that?"

"I told him if Annetje was going to hell I would be very happy to go with her and that it seemed to me a more congenial place than a realm populated by the likes of him."

"Was he angry?"

Dirk grinned. "He wanted to have me flogged but Jacop Hendricx, one of the ship's carpenters, saved me. He said I was a good apprentice and as long as I did my work he didn't care what I wore round my neck. In the end they let the matter drop."

Julie shook her head in bewilderment. What kind of a world was this, where ships could be stolen and men, women and children massacred in cold blood; where a sixteen year old boy could be flogged just for carrying a rosary? She shivered. What kind of a nightmare had she got herself into?

5

J ULIE WOKE to find morning sunshine filtering through the canvas of the little tent. She lay for some minutes with her eyes tightly closed, trying to convince herself that when she opened them she would be back on *Salamander* and none of the events of the previous night would really have happened. It did not work. She could feel the hard sand beneath her back and smell the roughly-cured sealskins that covered her. This place, this time, was a reality. Reluctantly she opened her eyes and, seeing she was alone, crawled to the door and peered out at the new day.

It was a crisp, cloudless morning. The inevitable southerly breeze fanned the surface of the lagoon into tiny ripples. A few finches darted among the bushes. Terns wheeled overhead. The basin, with its sand and reeds and spongy ground cover, looked exactly the same as when she and her father had explored it yesterday. Even the birds looked familiar. Had it not been for the tent and other signs of habitation it would have been easy to convince herself that she had been dreaming. But the tent was there and so were its occupants — or

48

one of them anyway. Dirk was at the fire stirring the remains of last night's stew, but there was no sign of the others. Julie went over to him. "Good morning," she said.

He lifted the ladle from the pot and held it out to her with a smile. "Good morning. Did you manage to sleep?"

"More or less." She sniffed the strong, fishy-smelling concoction and wrinkled her nose.

Dirk grinned. "You'd better get used to it. It's all we've got."

"Thanks," she said, "but I'm not really hungry. Where are the others?"

"Gone to look for driftwood." He put the ladle back in the pot and kicked sand over the ashes. "We daren't keep a fire going during the day," he explained. "They might see it."

Julie shivered. She stared incredulously round the island; it seemed so quiet — so normal — it was hard to imagine death lurking across the water.

"Do you really think they'll come back?" she asked.

"They hunt seals here," said Dirk. "They'll come; and eventually they are bound to spot us. Our only hope is to get to Soldiers Island."

"How much more have you got to do to the raft?"

"Come and see," he invited. They scrambled out of the sand basin and down the western slope of the ridge. The shoreline here was flat reef that hung out over the water in jagged ledges, but just further north the island narrowed and curved back in a small sandy bay. It was on this beach that the boys were building their raft. Julie examined it despondently. It was a clumsy looking thing, no more than a collection of flotsam, rudely lashed together, and pitifully small. It would need to be a lot bigger before it could support four of them. She turned and looked out towards the Wallabis. They appeared as one island at that distance, with the smaller shapes of Pigeon and Little Pigeon in the foreground. From West Wallabi a defiant plume of smoke curled up into the morning air.

"How far do you reckon it is?" she asked Dirk.

He narrowed his eyes, staring out across the water. "It's hard to tell. The light here plays tricks on you. We could make it though, with the right currents."

"On that?" Julie looked doubtfully at the unfinished raft.

Dirk shrugged. "Can you think of a better alternative?"

"No," she said. "I suppose not."

They stood in silence for a moment; then Dirk said: "We'd better go and look for the others and see if they've found anything useful." They walked back along the shore, neither of them speaking. An oyster-catcher was busy among the rocks. Its black head bobbed up and down as it dipped a bright red bill in and out of the crevices. Normally Julie would have delighted in it but today she barely noticed its existence. Her mind was consumed with the thought of that vast expanse of water and the pathetic little bundle of drift-wood. Could they really paddle it all the way to West Wallabi? Why was this happening to her? How had she got into this time and this murder-ridden nightmare?

A sharp cry shattered her thoughts. It sounded like a bird, but Dirk, at her side, stiffened and laid a hand on her arm and when it came again she knew it was human. She stared at him in horror.

"Quick!" he said. "Something's happened."

They ran up the slope, dropping instinctively to the ground as they neared the top, squirming through the brush on their bellies to peer over the crest. Julie stared across the half mile or so of water to Beacon Island — or *Batavia*'s Graveyard, as she must now learn to call it. Her eyes searched automatically for *Salamander*, but she was not there; neither was her jetty nor the smaller ones on the southern shore. And there were no huts, only a motley collection of tents. Oddly, despite all these differences, the island looked remarkably unchanged and its familiarity only added to her sense of dislocation. There were people on the shore, quite a crowd of them. They seemed to be gathered for some specific purpose and one of them was wearing what looked like a bright red coat.

Suddenly Julie realised they were all staring across the channel towards Long Island. At almost the same spot where she had brought the dinghy in last night a small boat bobbed up and down at the edge of the shallows. A man was standing in the water holding it. Three others stood on the shore. They were armed with cutlasses and huddled on the coral at their feet were Claas and Jan. Claas had his hands over his face and was wailing like a banshee; Jan was silent, staring at his captors in helpless terror. The men were laughing and their voices carried quite plainly up the slope. One of them prodded Claas in the ribs with his cutlass. "Where's the other one? Where's that little popish bastard?"

Claas wailed even louder. The man kicked him. "Answer me. We know he was here with you."

The boy began to babble, unintelligibly. Julie felt

Dirk's hand squeeze her shoulder. "Run!" he hissed. "Now!"

She slithered backwards till she was hidden by the slope and together they scrambled their way back to the little basin. Julie's heart was thumping like a jackhammer. "They'll search the island. What are we going to do? The raft?"

"There's no time. In here, quick!" He pulled aside the overhanging branches of a small bush on the slope of the basin. Julie saw that the earth beneath the roots had been scraped away to form a tiny cave. Obviously Dirk had been prepared for something like this. She squeezed in and he draped the branches back in front of her.

"What about you?"

He shook his head. "Just don't move," he said fiercely. "Whatever happens, don't move."

"But Dirk . . . "

"And don't speak! Remember, they don't know you're here."

Before she could argue he had moved away. From her hiding place she could see him standing by the ashes of the fire. He was making no attempt to hide. Suddenly she realised what his purpose was, and she tried to scream out to him to save himself, but the words died in her throat. Dirk's eyes swept the slope above her head. He stiffened. She heard the sound of footsteps pounding down the incline. Then at last he turned and fled.

He ran like a hunted deer, drawing the chase away from her hiding place. His bare feet splashed through the shallow water of the lake, followed by the heavier tread of his pursuer. Julie saw him scramble up the further side of the basin. He had almost reached the rim when another man loomed out of the scrub in front of him. Dirk tried to dodge, but his pursuer flung himself forward and grabbed him by one foot. Kicking and squirming, he was dragged back down the slope. At the last moment he managed to wrench himself free, but before he could roll away the second man was on him and had him pinned, face downward, with a knee in his back. His captors twisted his arms behind him, forcing his wrists up hard between his shoulder blades, and they laughed as he yelped with pain. When he struggled, one of them grabbed a handful of his hair and pushed his face down into the scrub.

Julie watched in horror. She thought they were going to smother him. His struggles gradually ceased and she could hear how he had to fight for every breath. At last, when he was quite still, the men relaxed their grip a little and he was able to turn his head sideways. He lay exhausted, breathing in long strangled gasps. When they finally pulled him to his feet again he sagged between them, unable even to stand unaided. The man who had chased him put a hand to his hair and lifted his head. Julie choked back a cry when she saw his face. It was covered in cuts and scratches and one eye was already half closed.

The man laughed. "Made quite a mess of his pretty face, haven't we! Take him to the beach and put him with the others. I'll be down in a minute."

His companion nodded. Holding Dirk's wrists clamped in one huge fist, he wrapped his other arm across the boy's chest and half dragged, half carried him up the slope. Dirk made no attempt to struggle; nor did he once look back.

The first man came back around the lake to the camp

site. Julie froze with terror but he made no attempt to search for her. He pulled down the makeshift tent and picked up the cooking pot and other odds and ends of equipment. Having secured his booty, he cast one final glance round the basin and then set off after his companion.

When he was safely out of sight Julie crawled from her hiding place. She was shaking with panic. Every instinct urged flight, but there was nowhere to run to. She felt abandoned. Where had they taken Dirk? What were they going to do to him? How would she survive without him? The terror of being left alone over-whelmed any other fear. She had to find out what was happening.

She wormed her way back to the top of the ridge, to a spot from where she could spy on the beach. Down on the shore Claas and Jan still sat hunched on the coral, under guard. Dirk had been dumped beside them. He lay sprawled on his back with his arms still twisted behind him; one of the men had a foot on his chest, holding him down. The man who had ransacked Dirk's camp site dropped his trophies at the water's edge and walked over to the little group. With his wild, black hair and bushy beard and a cutlass thrust through his belt, he looked like a pirate out of an adventure book — only this was no flight of fancy. This was real. He grinned down at his captives.

"Well, well! Three little rabbits for the pot. And a scrawny looking trio they are too." He looked at the man standing over Dirk. "What shall we do with them, Isbrant?"

Isbrant's reply was not loud enough for Julie to hear, but the meaning was quite unmistakable. He swung his sword in a great swishing arc above Dirk's face and roared with laughter as the boy jerked his head sideways. The black-haired pirate laughed also. He drew his own weapon and advanced gleefully on the petrified Claas. Claas howled with terror. He flung himself to his knees at the man's feet and clasped him around the knees.

"Don't kill me: ah, God, don't kill me!"

The man kicked him away contemptuously and stood over his prostrate body with upraised sword.

"No, please! I'll do anything. Anything!"

"Go on, Jacop," urged one of the others, "spit him through the belly and watch him squirm."

Jacop pretended to consider this for a moment; then suddenly he laughed. "No, I have a better idea." He leaned down and whispered something to the boy. Claas sobbed and shook his head violently. His captor shrugged and raised the sword again.

"All right; all right! I'll do it."

For a moment it seemed he had spoken too late, but at the last minute the poised muscles relaxed and the cutlass was thrust back into its makeshift scabbard. Jacop chuckled. "There now; I knew you would see reason. You do exactly as I say and I'll tell the Captain General what a good little boy you are." He reached down and hauled the youngster to his feet. "Now, let's take your companions back to the boat, shall we? And in case you are tempted to change your mind, remember you have an audience." And he waved a hand towards *Batavia*'s Graveyard.

The little procession moved down to the water. Julie watched them, sick with anxiety. Claas was weeping. Jan, who had sat in shock throughout the whole proceedings, moved like a sleepwalker, his face white and drained of any expression. Dirk struggled when they pulled him to his feet, though more from the pain in his arms than any real defiance. Isbrant swore at him and cuffed him across the head with his free hand. When they reached the boat he lifted the boy by his pinioned wrists and the waistband of his trousers, and threw him in headfirst. Julie winced as she imagined his unprotected face hitting the boards. The others scrambled over the gunwales. The man who had been minding the boat pushed it off with an oar and they moved out into the channel.

As she watched the boat pull away, Julie knew a moment of utter despair. It was all she could do not to rush down the beach after them and beg them not to leave her behind. She was close to hysteria. What would she do? How would she live? Who would ever come to rescue her? She had always prided herself on her toughness, but she felt about as tough now as a marshmallow. She longed for her family and the safety of familiar surroundings.

The little craft bobbed up and down on the swell. The oars dipped and rose and she could see the sailors leaning back into their strokes. Jan was sitting on the starboard gunwale, Claas on the port side. Dirk was still lying out of sight beneath the feet of the rowers. Suddenly, as if on an order, the men stopped rowing, and Julie knew with inexplicable certainty that something terrible was about to happen. The black-bearded Jacop leaned over and whispered something in Claas's ear. The boy stared around him wildly, then stood up and moved hesitantly across the boat. She saw him put his hands on Jan's shoulders.

"No!" Her throat contracted as though in a howl of pain, but it was Jan who cried; one long, heart-stopping scream that echoed across the sky and drowned in a flurry of churning water. She heard the laughter of his murderers. They nudged the board forward, just enough to put it beyond his reach, and watched until the threshing and flailing ceased and the sea was calm once more. Then they looked again at Claas.

Julie put her hands over her face. She knew what must happen next and could not bear to watch it. In the end, though, she had to look: imagining was worse than seeing. Dirk put up a tremendous fight. He was older than Claas and, despite the rough handling he had received, more than a match for him. The boat rocked wildly as they struggled and for a moment Julie thought they would both go over the side. The men leaned on their oars and watched them; she could hear them laughing and shouting encouragement. Finally Jacop put an end to it. Almost casually, he leaned forward and fetched Dirk a clout across the head that dropped him to the boards. Before he could rise, Claas had seized him by one arm and leg and Isbrant by the other. They swung him forward and back a couple of times and then, to a mighty cheer from all the rowers, heaved him out over the side. His body soared through the air, a fountain of spray shot upwards as it hit the water, and then — nothing. He sank like a stone.

Jacop turned to face Batavia's Graveyard and raised one clenched fish in a grim salute. It was echoed by the red-clad figure on the beach. The sailors bent to their oars again. One of them began to sing. Claas sat between Jacop and Isbrant, his face buried in his hands, and Julie knew that he was crying.

6

SLOWLY, as in a dream, Julie walked back to the deserted camp. She sat on the patch of sand where the tent had been, her arms clasped around her knees, and stared unseeingly at the ripples on the lake. "He's gone," she said to herself. "Dirk is dead. They took him away in the boat and they drowned him. He's dead." The words sounded flat and unreal. She repeated them over and over again, trying to draw some sense of grief from them, but nothing came: they were just words; meaningless. She went on staring at the water.

The sun climbed towards noon. Its rays caught the white, salt crust round the edge of the lake and set it sparkling. A seagull strutted across the sand, leaving little arrowhead prints along the shoreline; a small crab scuttled out from under a piece of coral and made a dash for the water. Julie didn't move. She sat, cold and remote as a statue, and watched her empty world with brittle calmness. At last something caught her eye on the far shore of the lake: something black and shiny that glittered as it caught the sunlight. She stood up and, with slow, deliberate steps, walked over to it. She picked it up. It was a string of black glass beads — Dirk's rosary. The chain was broken. It must have snapped in his struggle with his murderers. She hooked it together again and pinched the link shut with her teeth. The beads were warm from the sunshine; before, they would have held the warmth of Dirk's body.

He's dead, she thought, Dirk is dead, and this is his rosary. The beads felt reassuringly familiar in her hands. She slid them through her fingers one by one, reciting mechanically: *"Our Father, who art in heaven... Hail Mary, full of grace, the Lord is with thee... Holy Mary, mother of God, pray for us sinners now and at the hour of our death. Amen"*... The hour of our death... An image blazed through her mind of that slim figure falling through the air. She saw the sea open to receive him, the sheet of spray, the silence as it closed about his body. *Now and at the hour of our death.* Dirk was dead; gone for ever. Overwhelmed by the realisation, she dropped to the ground and abandoned herself to grief. She cried until, exhausted, she fell asleep.

When she woke the sun was already low and the warmth had gone from the little basin. She rubbed her eyes and sat up. Fear and grief crept back into her heart, but at least now that terrible numbness had gone. She could think again and she knew what she had to do. "They hunt seals here," Dirk had said. "Our only hope is to get to Soldiers Island." She must take her chances on the raft. It had been too flimsy for four, but it might carry one safely. She would have to risk it. And she must go soon, today if possible. There was always the chance Claas might tell Cornelisz about her.

59

Dirk's rosary was still twined about her fingers. She put it round her neck and tucked it underneath her shirt; then she made her way down to the little bay. There were seals on the beach, about half a dozen of them — childlike creatures with fawn backs and cream-coloured bellies and huge velvety eyes. They watched her suspiciously as she came along the shore and lumbered off into the water long before she got close to them. Their experience of the human race had not been one to inspire trust. The raft still lay where she and Dirk had examined it that morning. A second inspection proved no more encouraging than the first. The ropes which bound it together were frayed and rotting and the whole contraption looked as if it would fall apart the minute it was put into the water. Her heart sank. She looked across at West Wallabi island and tried to imagine herself safely ashore there, but the more she thought about it the more fearful she grew.

It was growing late, too. If she tried to make the crossing this evening it would be dark before she got there, and if the raft broke up and she had to swim . . . She remembered the sharks she had hooked on snapper lines at about this time in the evening and her father's strict rule: no diving after four o'clock. No, to leave now would be sheer lunacy. Even if Claas had betrayed her to the mutineers it was unlikely they would come back for her tonight. She would go in the morning, at first light, but, just to be on the safe side, she would stay well away from the camp site and keep a constant watch on *Batavia*'s Graveyard.

Once more she made her way up the spine-like ridge of the island, this time keeping well north of the little basin. The terns rose screeching before her, and she cursed them; she would have to be very careful not to disturb them after nightfall or they would give her away for sure. She wondered guiltily if it had been her blundering around last night that had betrayed the boys. Once the birds had settled again the island seemed horribly deserted. A pair of Pacific gulls, their heads turned stoically into the wind, stood sentinel near the spot where the mutineers had come ashore. Further along the beach a lone seal lay sleeping at the water's edge; its form looked almost human in the fading light. The sun was like a streak of blood behind the Wallabis. *Batavia*'s Graveyard, with its coral shores and stunted vegetation and little shanty town of canvas, was already blurring into silhouette.

The evening breeze had a chilling bite to it. Julie shivered in her prickly nest and fought back the misery that threatened to engulf her. She began to play dangerous games with herself. If I shut my eyes, when I open them again I'll see the jetty and *Salamander* and Ian's boat tied up behind her. If I put my hands over my ears then when I take them away again I'll hear Dad coming over in the dinghy to look for me. But there was nothing: only the sea and the wind and the restless cries of the terns. When she looked again, the gulls had gone.

It was too dark now to see anything clearly beyond the shoreline. Even the sleeping seal was no more than a vague black shape. As she watched it, it stirred and began to inch its way up the beach. It moved so slowly and so awkwardly she wondered if it was injured. Perhaps it had been speared by one of the castaways. The thought reminded her how hungry she was; and thirsty; she had had nothing to eat or drink all day. Why had she not taken the soup Dirk had offered her? Could she really have considered it unpleasant? She could taste it now in her mind and remember the smell of it and it seemed to her the most delicious aroma in the world. She sat up, hugging her empty belly and feeling very sorry for herself.

The seal had stopped moving and lay slumped on the beach, a forlorn grey figure against the bleached coral. She wondered if it was dead. There was something very odd about it. In the half-light you could almost imagine . . . Suddenly she started, her hands pressed to her mouth to stifle a cry. It couldn't be . . . it simply couldn't be . . . But her eyes, straining into the shadows, caught the unmistakable flutter of cloth about the still form and a ruffling of hair. It was Dirk!

Oblivious to all need for caution, she scrambled to her feet and ran down the beach, her feet slithering and stumbling among the coral clinkers. She flung herself to her knees beside the unconscious figure and rolled it gently onto its back. The thin, gaunt face was battered almost beyond recognition, the eyes closed, the breath a laboured rattle in the back of the throat. His skin was as cold and clammy as death. She seized him by the shoulders and shook him. "Dirk, oh Dirk! Wake up! Speak to me!"

The long lashes fluttered weakly. A tear crept from the corner of one eye and trickled down a bruised cheek; the lips moved. "Annetje?" The words slid off into a fit of coughing. Dirk's thin body jerked in convulsive spasms. He began to vomit.

Julie scooped him into her arms and clutched him against her fiercely. "Oh Dirk, you're not going to die! You're not, you're not! I won't let you!"

For what seemed an eternity she sat on the coral and

rocked the half-drowned boy in her arms while he threshed and gasped and spewed up seawater. She was appalled by the violence of his vomiting. Sometimes the convulsions lasted so long she was sure he would suffocate; afterwards he would catch his breath in huge, straining gasps that she thought must tear his lungs apart. She was frantic at her own helplessness. Several times she almost wished he would die; anything to put an end to his suffering. But he fought on with relentless determination, long after the last of his strength had gone.

At last he had cleaned himself out. Little by little the cramped belly muscles softened and relaxed and his breathing settled back into a normal rhythm. Finally, with a little sob, his head fell back against Julie's shoulder and he slept. Julie, too, was exhausted. She bowed her face into the thick salt-tasting hair and wept. She stroked his head and rocked him in her arms like a baby, and as she listened to the regular rise and fall of his breath her heart thumped with triumph and relief. He was safe; they were both safe. Together they had faced death and they had conquered it. They had survived.

For maybe three hours she sat and cradled him, but the night air was growing colder all the time and eventually she realised she was going to have to find some shelter for them both. She tried to rouse him and eventually he stirred in her arms and opened his eyes. He was shivering and his teeth chattered violently as he tried to speak. "Cold," he whispered, "... so cold."

She held him closely. "I know. I have to get you out of this wind. Do you think you can walk if I help you?"

He nodded. Slowly and with difficulty she got him to his feet and, with his arm draped across her shoulders and hers around his waist, supported him as they stumbled back to the salt lake. She knew they were taking a risk going back there but it was the only protected spot she could think of. Dirk was exhausted when they finally slid down the steep, northern side of the little basin. He lay shivering on the sand beside the old camp fire and Julie stripped off her jumper and pulled it over his head. She put her socks on his bare feet and made him curl up as small as possible; then she huddled against him, trying to warm him with the heat of her own body.

It did little good, for she was already cold herself. After a few moments he lifted his head and said through chattering teeth: "No use . . . have to risk . . . fire."

"But how?" wailed Julie, who would have sold her soul at that moment for just one handful of burning twigs. "We've go nothing to light it with."

"Behind that bush," Dirk mumbled, pointing. " . . . For the raft."

Julie went over to the bush he indicated and groped behind the overhanging foliage. Her fingers closed on fabric and after a brief effort she pulled out a large canvas sack. She dragged it across to Dirk and unpacked it in front of him: two flasks of water, a box of hard biscuits, a couple of blankets and — "What's this?" she asked, opening a small wooden box and staring in puzzlement at the contents. She prodded them with a finger: a stone, a small bar of steel and a quantity of coarse fibre that looked like roughly carded wool. She held the box out to Dirk. "What is it?" she asked again.

"A *tondeldoos*," said Dirk.

"A what?" Julie stared at him blankly. She had never even heard the word before.

"A *tondeldoos*; to make fire."

Comprehension dawned. A tinderbox! "Oh," she said. She turned the box reverently in her hands and images leapt into her mind of red-coated soldiers and dogs with eyes as big as saucers.

In the ashes of the old camp fire they built the foundations of their new one. Julie had to do most of the hard work, for Dirk was still too weak to stand. She scouted around patiently in the dark for anything that would burn and when at last she had collected sufficient brushwood for a fire he showed her how to light it. As she watched, he emptied onto the ground a little of the fibrous material from the box: it was linen, he told her, impregnated with saltpetre. Then he built around it a little cradle of dry twigs. Finally he took the flintstone and the steel and began to strike them together over the tinder to make a spark. His hands were clumsy with cold and exhaustion, and he had to do it many times before the linen ignited, but finally a tiny flame licked upwards. He fanned it gently with his breath, adding twigs to it one by one until at last the whole cradle was on fire; then bit by bit he built it up with larger pieces until eventually it was crackling merrily and throwing out life-saving warmth.

They curled up in front of it like a couple of cats. Dirk's eyes closed again. He still looked dreadfully ill and Julie wished desperately that the morning would come. She stripped off his wet clothes and spread them out near the fire to dry. She tucked both the blankets around him and folded her jumper to make a pillow; then she settled down beside him to tend the fire and keep watch over him while he slept. She was too hungry to sleep and, as she sat there staring into the fire, she suddenly remembered the biscuits and the water. Eagerly she fetched them. The biscuits were so hard they were almost impossible to chew, but she poured water over them, using a flat piece of coral as a plate, and allowed them to stand for a while to soften up. They swelled considerably as they soaked up the water and two of them made a surprisingly satisfying meal. Once she had eased her own hunger she set about preparing some for Dirk. She let them soak till they were mushy and stirred them into a sloppy porridge with a twig; then she put her coral plate among the ashes and let it warm a little. When it was ready she woke Dirk and fed him, a very little at a time, using her fingers as a spoon.

She was afraid it might make him sick again but, to her relief, he managed to keep it down; it seemed to help him. When it was all gone he smiled and stretched contentedly and went back to sleep — if, indeed, he had ever been properly awake.

Making herself as comfortable as possible, she resumed her vigil, with every intention of remaining awake all night, but as the hours passed her eyelids grew heavier and heavier. For a long time she struggled to keep them from closing but eventually she opened them to find the morning sun shining on her face and realised she had been sound asleep. Instinctively she turned to check on Dirk and saw that his sleeping place was empty. She sat up in panic.

"It's all right," said a now familiar voice. "There's no danger. I just checked the channel and there's not a boat in sight."

Dirk was standing by the fire, fully dressed, poking something in the ashes. He looked terrible. His face was covered in cuts and scratches, both eyes had been blackened and one was so swollen it had disappeared in a mass of bruising. There were bruises round his wrists too, and his shirt hung from his back in ribbons. But he was alive, and, astonishingly, seemed little the worse for his ordeal. He grinned when he saw the consternation in her face and, stooping, lifted one of her coral plates out of the ashes. "Breakfast," he said. "Rock crabs; but you'll have to be careful, they're very hot." He sat down beside her and together they shared his meagre offering, cracking the little shells with their teeth and sucking out the morsels of roasted flesh. Julie thought she had never tasted a more delicious meal in her life. She licked the last crumbs from her fingers with a regretful sigh. "That was beautiful," she said. "You're very resourceful, Dirk. I'd never have thought of catching them."

"You would," he assured her, "if you'd been as hungry as I've been." He laughed, and winced as a cut at the corner of his mouth began to bleed again.

She put a hand to his cheek. "Oh, Dirk, your poor face. They really made a mess of you, didn't they? Is it very painful?"

He smiled again, wryly. "It's better than being dead."

Julie shivered. She remembered again her anguish of the previous day. "I thought you *were* dead. Oh, Dirk, it was horrible. I really thought they'd drowned you."

"Not me," said Dirk. "They should have known better. I was born in a caul; I'll never drown. But poor little Jan was not so lucky. He must have gone straight to the bottom. I tried to find him but it was hopeless. They'd banged me over the head so many times I hardly knew what I was doing. I kept passing out and I must have swallowed lots of seawater."

67

"You did," said Julie. "I thought you were going to kill yourself bringing it all up again. I don't think I've ever been so frightened in my life."

He hugged her compassionately. "If you hadn't found me I probably would have died. I'd never have lasted the night down there on the beach in wet clothes."

"How could he do it?" she demanded angrily. "He was supposed to be your friend; how could he do it to you?"

"Claas?" Dirk shook his head sadly. "How could he refuse? If he had they'd only have made Jan do it — or me."

"Not you, Dirk. You'd never do a thing like that, I know you wouldn't."

"Do you? Then you know more than I do," said Dirk abruptly. He stood up and kicked sand over the fire. "I don't want to talk about it any more. Come on, we'd better get all this stuff down to the raft and move out before someone decides to come and check the island again."

They repacked the sack and Julie followed him down to the little bay in silence. His words had shocked her and the more she thought about them the more guilty and uncomfortable she felt. Suppose she had been in that boat; suppose she had been the one ordered to murder her companions: what kind of a response would she have made? It was a question she didn't want to answer.

7

WHEN THEY got down to the beach Julie's courage almost failed her. West Wallabi island seemed even further away than it had yesterday and the sea looked grey and angry. The rain-scented wind was blowing harder than ever. The only slight consolation was that it had shifted a few degrees further east and would assist them in their crossing. She looked at the flimsy raft and then at Dirk and saw her fears mirrored in his face. His hand went to the front of his shirt as though seeking something, and she remembered the rosary. She pulled it off and held it out to him. "Here, I found it by the lake."

He reached for it eagerly, but then hesitated. "Are you sure you wouldn't rather keep it?"

She looked at it for a moment, turning it in her hands, feeling its warmth between her fingers; then she slipped it gently over his head. "No, it's yours; you wear it — for both of us."

"Thank you." He smiled at her almost shyly and touched the crucifix to his lips before tucking it back under the remains of his shirt. "Annetje would have liked you," he said, and she knew he could have paid her no higher compliment.

Together they dragged the raft down to the water. Afloat, it inspired even less confidence than it had on the beach — it bobbed up and down like a drunken duck in the shallow water. Julie cast one last glance around the little island, which now seemed cosy and familiar, and steeled herself for the ordeal ahead. Dirk heaved the sack aboard and lashed it down with a piece of rope. He looked at Julie. "Well; shall we go?"

She nodded. In silence they pushed their little vessel out through the shallows and climbed aboard. It sagged alarmingly beneath their weight; waves slopped over the top of it and ran out between the boards. They lay side by side, clinging to the ropes which bound it together. There was no hope of steering it in these seas; they would have to trust to the mercy of the currents. It was going to be a long, wet voyage.

It was also a rough voyage. Julie had never imagined how exhausting it would be simply trying to stay on the raft. It bounced up and down in the heavy seas, rising with the waves and dropping back into the troughs with a gut-wrenching crash, flinging them about, like buck-jumpers at a rodeo. Before long her shoulders arched and her arms felt as though they were being torn from their sockets; and to all these miseries was soon added another one, nausea: half an hour of constant pounding, and Julie, who had never been seasick in her life, was retching helplessly. Dirk tried to comfort her but he was in little better state himself and too engrossed in his own struggle to be of much help to her.

Before long she had lost all sense of time and place.

Nothing existed but that rough, soggy bundle of drift-wood. It seemed as though there had been no moment of her existence when she had not been clinging to it and no moment when she would cease to do so. There was no past, no future; only pain and sickness and eternal misery. It was beyond endurance and it was pointless. Quite suddenly she saw how ridiculous it was — and how easily she could make an end to it. With a sob of relief she loosened her grip on the ropes and the next wave lifted her and washed her gently from the raft. The water rose to claim her and swallowed her in the vast, green wetness of its throat. She sank, unresisting.

A hand grabbed her wrist; and a voice shouted in her ear; she tried to tear herself away. The wind and sea sucked at her body, dragging her down to oblivion, but the hand would not relinquish her. "Let me go! Let me go!" she screamed, but it clung remorselessly. Gradually Dirk pulled her back onto the raft and, when she continued to struggle, released her arm and hit her hard across the face. She collapsed sobbing. He rolled across her and pinned her down on the raft with his own weight. She kicked and screamed but he held her doggedly, half smothering her beneath his body as his hands clung to the ropes on either side of her. At last she had nothing left to fight with. She flopped, exhausted, and the madness slowly drained from her body. It was replaced by apathy. Why bother? She could change nothing: neither life, nor death nor even the constant sickness. In the hands of fate, she was utterly powerless. As she drifted into semi-consciousness, strange dreams chased each other through her mind, tumbling over themselves in a kaleidoscope of memories and impressions.

71

How long she remained in this state she never knew but, suddenly, she snapped out of it to find herself in the water again, choking and floundering, swirling in a maelstrom of boiling surf, and Dirk's voice was screaming in her ear: "Swim, Julie, swim!" Her arms and legs obeyed instinctively. Threshing and kicking, she clawed her way through the churning waves until suddenly she saw in front of her a ledge of rock. Her hands latched onto it and clung like limpets while the sea pounded and sucked at her body as though in a frenzy to dislodge her. Through the spray she saw Dirk trying to haul himself out of the water. Three times it caught him and dragged him back again, but at last he heaved himself clear and fell, sprawling, on the flat ledge.

He lay there for a moment, gasping helplessly. Then he squirmed forward and she felt his hands grasp her under the shoulders. "Kick!" he commanded, his voice a shrill scream above the thundering surf. She threshed desperately, trying to drive her body upwards. Dirk dragged her shoulders over the edge. "Again!" he shouted. One hand slid down her back and grabbed the waistband of her jeans and as she kicked again he heaved her upwards. Her chest and belly scraped painfully across the jagged coral, her legs flailed wildly as they left the water, and at last she was lying on flat coral-rock, hawking up seawater and sucking great lungfuls of air into her oxygen-starved body.

Dirk had collapsed beside her, equally exhausted. For a long time they both lay without moving; then, slowly, Julie reached out her hand and let it rest on Dirk's back. She could feel the rise and fall of his ribs as he breathed. "We did it!" she whispered. "Oh Dirk, we did it!"

He rolled over to look at her. "Didn't I tell you I was never born to drown?" He grinned. "Though I confess I had a few anxious moments when the raft broke up. Thank God you can swim so well. Wherever did you learn?"

"Oh, here and there," said Julie awkwardly. She felt shy talking about her own life; it hardly seemed real any longer. "Where are we?" she asked, changing the subject. "Is this Soldiers Island?"

He shook his head. "No, this one has no name. It lies between Seals Island and Soldiers Island."

Julie sat up in sudden panic. "Is it safe?"

"Yes," he said. "No-one comes here, as far as I know. But it means our journey is not yet over. We shall have to swim the rest of the way."

Julie stared at him bleakly. She rolled over and buried her head in her arms. "I can't, Dirk. I just can't."

"Yes you can. We don't have to go immediately; we'll rest first. And we'll be in sheltered water from now on."

"No," she said, and she burrowed her face deeper into the protection of her arms. "No, I can't do it."

He didn't argue with her, and she continued to lie face downwards on the hard coral, refusing to look at him, shivering with cold in her wet clothes. After a while she felt his hand on her shoulder. "We'll catch a chill if we stay here. Let's try and find a bit of shelter."

Reluctantly she allowed him to help her to her feet, and they set out to explore the island. It was as bleak and bare as all the others, but the jagged coral of the western shoreline dropped away almost like small cliffs in places and there were little crannies which offered shelter from the wind. From this side of the island, West Wallabi — Soldiers Island — looked big and friendly and tantalisingly close. There were a couple of smaller islands, too, that were even nearer, and the sea around them was certainly much calmer, but still Julie's heart failed her when she thought of trying to reach them. She simply could not do it: not for Dirk; not for anyone. Even had Cornelisz himself been standing behind her with a cutlass in his hand there was no way she could have made herself go back into the water.

Dirk must have realised how she felt, for he made no further effort to persuade her. He found a cleft in the rock face, above the tideline and just big enough for them both to squeeze into, and when they had crawled into it and were out of the wind, he told her she should try to sleep. Julie thought he was crazy. How could anyone sleep who was so cold and scared and miserable? She thought wistfully of the sack that had gone down with the raft and longed for the warmth of those blankets. Above all, and quite inappropriately, she grieved for the loss of the tinderbox. It was nothing to do with their need for fire, simply for the intrinsic beauty of the thing and the sense of wonder it had evoked in her when she first saw it. She felt as though some magic talisman had been taken from her. For a while she lay shivering in her wet clothes, nursing her miseries, but in the end, despite herself, she dropped into a deep sleep, curled up like an orphaned kitten in the shelter of Dirk's arms.

She was sitting by the barbecue at home. It was crackling brightly and she could smell the steak sizzling on the hotplate. There was a big salad bowl in her lap and she was pulling a lettuce apart and dropping the pieces into the bowl. Her hands were cold, for the lettuce was wet and soggy, but however quickly she tore the leaves from it, it never seemed to grow any smaller. She wanted to push it away but she knew that until it was all prepared no-one would be able to eat, and she was hungry. Her father and Paul were talking somewhere behind her. They seemed to be worried about her and to think she was asleep. She tried to tell them that she wasn't. They were bending over her; calling to her, asking her what was wrong. She tried to say she was all right but her voice seemed frozen in her throat — she strained and strained but nothing would come; not even a squeak. Her father put a hand on her shoulder and shook her.

Her voice erupted in a strangled shout which jolted her back to reality. She was cramped and cold, scrunched between two walls of rock, unable to move. A huge, rough, red-bearded face was looming over her, consuming her whole field of vision. She screamed. The face swooped closer. Her hands shot up instinctively, clawing and scratching like a trapped animal. A pair of hands caught her wrists. She struggled, hysterical with terror, screaming for Dirk. The hands pulled her upward, strong arms engulfed her in a bear-hug, her face was pressed against a broad, warm chest. A voice said in her ear: "Annetje, don't be frightened. It's me, *kindje*; it's Weibbe Hayes." Fear and strength drained from her body simultaneously; the nightmare fled in a long, bewildered wail, and she slid into blackness.

The next few hours were a jumble of confused impressions: arms, hands, the rocking motion of a boat; food and friendly voices, and the soft, unbelievable luxury of warmth. She woke once, frightened and calling for Dirk, and a voice said: "He's here, beside you." She turned her head and saw him, sleeping peacefully, his thin figure swathed in a motley collection of rugs and skins. She reached out for him and someone took his hand and put it into hers. She smiled and went back to sleep.

When she woke again it was dark; there was a smell of cooking and the air was vibrant with the sound of voices. She opened her eyes and peered around her in bewilderment. She was in a small, stone-walled enclosure. There was no roof, but above the corner where she was lying some skins had been stretched over a frame, in lean-to fashion, to afford a little protection in case of rain. The place was full of people and they all seemed to be eating. Confused and a little frightened, she looked around anxiously for Dirk. He was sitting against the far wall, drinking something from a large shell. There was steam rising from it and it made Julie's mouth water just to look at it. Beside Dirk was a man whose face she recognised; it was the face that had so terrified her earlier in the day. Seen now, in an atmosphere of warmth and safety, it was a friendly face: plain and honest and reassuringly forthright. It reminded her a bit of her father. She sat up and, when he saw she was awake, the man came over, bringing with him a steaming shell, similar to Dirk's. He held it out to her and his weather-beaten face crinkled into a grin. "So, our sleeping princess is awake again. How do you feel?"

"Hungry," she said gratefully. She took the shell and sniffed the contents. It gave off a delicious, meaty aroma.

"What is it?"

"Stewed cat."

"Cat?" She almost dropped the shell in her horror. Hayes roared with laughter.

"No, no, *meisje*, have no fear; these are not your little,

household pussycats. They are wild creatures: small, hopping beasts with pouches in their bellies to carry their young. You have their skins for your blankets."

Wallabies! Julie stroked the brown furry rug across her knees and laughed. Of course, these people had never seen such creatures before. How would they know what name to give them? She polished off the broth, fishing the chunks of meat out with her fingers, and it tasted every bit as good as it smelled.

While she was eating, Dirk came over to sit beside her. He looked very pale and tired and she felt ashamed of herself for the hard time she had given him.

"I'm sorry," she said. "I wasn't much help, was I?"

"Nonsense," he assured her gallantly. "It's not your fault. This must be even more terrifying for you than for the rest of us. After all, you don't even belong here." He frowned suddenly and dropped his voice. "Julie, there are going to be difficulties. I had not thought ... "

Before he could finish his sentence a burly man pushed his way between them and, beaming from ear to ear, bent over Julie and kissed her soundly on both cheeks. "*Alors, ma p'tite,*" he boomed, and went off into a long string of incomprehensible language. Julie stared at him in horror. My God, she thought, he's speaking French and I'm supposed to understand him. He thinks I'm Anne-Marie. She turned panic-stricken eyes on Dirk, but he was powerless to help her. The man had apparently asked her a question, for he stood with hands on hips, looking down at her and smiling in faint puzzlement at her obvious incomprehension. She was numb with terror, she stuttered, her jaw trembled. Not knowing what to do, she dropped her face into her hands and burst into tears.

There was an instant's silence, then a babble of concerned voices began shouting, all at once, in a confusion of French and Dutch. Suddenly Dirk's voice cut across them: calm, polite, eloquent, with sheer inspiration. "I'm sorry, Jean, but I don't think she understands you. You see, she doesn't remember anything."

The voices ceased abruptly. "What do you mean: she doesn't remember anything?" someone asked. "What has she forgotten?"

"Everything," said Dirk, warming to his tale. "The wreck, her father's death, how she got ashore. When I found her on Seals Island she couldn't even remember who she was." He put an arm round Julie's shoulder and squeezed her reassuringly. "It must have been the shock. God knows, what we've been through would be enough to addle anyone's brains."

"But how could she possibly forget her own language?" asked the man called Jean, in bewilderment.

"I don't know," said Dirk, "but she has; and she's certainly forgotten your faces. You ask Weibbe."

"It's true," said Hayes. "She thought I was one of Cornelisz's cronies. She tried to scratch my eyes out." He put a hand under Julie's chin and lifted her tear-stained face to his own. His blue eyes twinkled down at her compassionately. "Don't you be scared, little one. You're safe here with us and in time it will all come back to you. I've seen it happen before, on the battlefield; it passes." He patted her on the shoulder. "Now, you curl up and have a good night's sleep and in the morning you'll be as chirpy as a sparrow again."

He took the empty shell from her lap and shooed everyone away, leaving her alone with her champion.

She snuggled down under the wallaby skins and giggled sleepily as Dirk tucked them round her shoulders.

"Oh. Dirk, you were brilliant, absolutely brilliant."

He kissed his fingertips and touched them gently to her cheek. "Go to sleep," he said.

8

THE NEXT DAY was taken up with exploring their new surroundings and, in Julie's case, getting to know her companions. This was a slightly unnerving experience, for she was well aware how odd it must seem to them that she should not remember either their names or faces. Several of the soldiers were French and had been close friends of Anne-Marie's father. She could sense their discomfort at having to converse with her in broken Dutch. A few of them looked at her strangely but if they had reservations about her story they never voiced them. Weibbe Hayes had made it clear she was not to be questioned and his word, it seemed, was law.

Soldiers Island had more to offer than any of the others in the group. It was bigger, and the landscape was more interesting. There were bushes, even a few stunted trees, areas of thick ground cover, flat, sandy plains and outcrops of rock — real limestone rock, not merely chunks of dead coral. The bird life also was more varied: apart from the ubiquitous terns and mutton birds, there were several mainland species — finches and bronzewing pigeons and even wedge-tailed eagles. But most incredible of all were the wallabies. Even though she knew of their existence, Julie could still hardly believe her eyes when she saw them. They seemed so out of place in this strange setting. They were small dainty creatures with cat-like faces and huge ears that twitched at the slightest sound. It seemed tragic that they had to be killed and Julie felt a little guilty when she remembered how she had enjoyed her stew the previous evening, but she knew it was a question of necessity and, after all, the fish and birds and gentle, soft-eyed seals, whose flesh also went to fill the cooking pots, were no less beautiful or deserving of life.

Weibbe Hayes showed them over his little domain with pride. He explained how he and his men had collected coral flags to build their shelters — 'our forts' he called them — and showed them the wells they had never been meant to find. The cooks of each day had the task of carting water to the camp and Julie could understand why it was a job nobody wanted. The main well was far from the camp site and the ground in between was riddled with mutton-bird burrows. There was absolutely no way of telling whether the spot where you were about to place your foot was solid ground or the thin roof of a bird's nest and she and Dirk had laughed uproariously as they sank, almost to their knees at times, in soft sand, dragging themselves out only to collapse again with astonished yelps a few seconds later. They might find it funny but, for a weary man lugging a barrel of water, the experience would be anything but amusing.

"Still," said Hayes, with a chuckle, "at least we know

they are there. Anyone coming ashore at night and trying to creep up on our forts would be in for a rude awakening."

"Are you expecting visitors?" asked Dirk.

Hayes grinned. "We've had one already. Haven't you met him yet?"

When they both shook their heads Hayes laughed again and led them to his second fort. It was closer to the beach than the one in which they had slept the previous night, and was guarded by three men armed with rough-hewn but very substantial-looking clubs. In one corner, bound hand and foot and looking very sorry for himself, was a young man whose tattered finery proclaimed a background somewhat more exalted than that of his captors. He scowled when he saw Hayes and let fly with a string of invective. Hayes ignored it but one of the others leaned across the wall and silenced him with a casual backhander across the mouth.

Dirk blinked at him in astonishment. "Daniel Cornelissen," he said at last.

"Yes," agreed Hayes. "Daniel Cornelissen, nobleman and naval cadet — and as nasty a piece of work as ever walked God's earth. Didn't you know he was one of Cornelisz's pets?"

Dirk shook his head.

"He arrived three days ago," continued Hayes, "with a letter from his master. Addressed to the French soldiers, it was, and fairly dripping with honey. '*Beloved brothers and friends... We wonder that you who left willingly to survey the High island do not return to bring us word.*' Return indeed! After they had left us here without a boat! '*We think it strange you give hearing to the tale-bearing of some evildoers who were sent by us to*

another island but came here without our knowledge.'
That's you two he's talking about, and young Cornelis
Jansz and the few others who escaped his massacres.
*'Come to us, help us, give into our hands those who so
treacherously robbed us of our little yawl.'* Some robber!
Aris Jansz, who arrived here a week ago, still bleeding
from the wounds they gave him when they enticed him
down to the beach at night and tried to cut his throat!
My God, the man must think us complete fools."
Hayes's leathery features flushed to a dark red and he
turned on his captive a scowl of such ferocious indignation the young man averted his eyes and shrank back
against the wall.

"I don't know why you bother with him," said one of
his guards. "If I had my way I'd show him the same
mercy his friends showed young Dirk here, only I'd
make sure he was bound hand and foot first and I'd tie a
sack of rocks round his neck for good measure."

"No," said Hayes. "I'm not going to sink to their
level. He'll get a fair hearing when the time comes."

"*If* it comes," said the man gloomily. "It's my belief
we're doomed to die here. Don't forget Aarian Jacobz
and his boatswain are both in that boat with Pelsaert
and they were two of the chief ringleaders in the
mutiny plot. They've probably thrown him overboard
by now."

"Even if they have," Hayes consoled him, "they still
have to make landfall somewhere, and Batavia's the
closest port."

"Suppose they simply tell the Company there are no
other survivors."

Hayes chuckled. "They'd still send someone to find
the wreck. Men may be expendable, but not all that

gold! Besides, there are forty men in Pelsaert's boat. They can't all be liars."

"Well, I hope you're right," said the man, but he didn't sound altogether convinced.

Hayes and the two youngsters walked back to the camp. It had started to rain and Dirk shivered in his tattered clothes. The soldiers had given him wallaby skins to wrap around his legs and shoulders but they were roughly cured and stiff and uncomfortable to wear. "Warmth is our biggest problem," Hayes had told them. "We have all the food and water we need but I'd give my right arm for some good clothes and a few decent tents and blankets."

Julie felt thankful for her own denim jeans and thick sweater. They were stiff with salt and beginning to smell, but they certainly kept out the cold. She had seen the others staring at them from time to time and knew they found her appearance quite strange. Dirk had spun them some tale of her having found them in one of the chests salvaged from the ship and, since no-one liked to question her, they had to be satisfied with that explanation.

The camp site was a hive of activity. There were men cooking, men cleaning skins, men making clogs and wooden utensils and manufacturing vicious looking weapons out of bits of flotsam and rusty nails. Hayes had worked miracles with his little band and was certainly not going to be taken by surprise. Down by the shore some of the soldiers were gathering coral flags and stacking them in strategic piles around the small bay, through which any invaders would have to approach the island. "Ammunition," said Hayes with a grin when Julie questioned him. "Crude but very effective. The water's quite shallow round here so it's a long walk ashore: with a crowd of desperate men pelting rocks at you as you came it could be downright uncomfortable." Julie gazed out across the churning water. From here you could not even see *Batavia*'s Graveyard. Surely no-one in his right mind would venture so far in an open boat in this weather. Then she remembered the trip she and Dirk had made on the raft; she shivered. How had they ever survived?

"Which is the island we landed on?" she asked.

Hayes pointed. "Over there," he said. "You were lucky we found you. We don't usually bother with those islands; but when we saw all the birds agitated we thought it might have been some of Cornelissen's cronies come looking for him, so we decided to investigate."

"Thank God you did," said Dirk fervently. "I don't think we could have gone any further."

The wind blew itself out during the night and the morning dawned bright and sunny — one of those perfect Abrolhos days. Julie was delighted, but Weibbe Hayes set a double watch on the coast and from time to time went down to the bay himself to scan the horizon with anxious blue eyes. If the weather favoured them it would also favour any would-be attackers.

Dirk was making himself a pair of clogs. He had offered to make some for Julie but she had declined, preferring to stick with her old sneakers. Her Dutch grandmother had once sent her a pair of clogs and she still remembered the blisters they had given her. She sat in the sunshine watching Dirk as he worked, admiring his patience and the deftness of his hands as they carved and shaped the stubborn wood. He had told her, she recalled, that he was a carpenter's apprentice. Julie was useless at finicky work: she loved to paint but she splashed her colours across the canvas in fierce, sweeping strokes and very rarely finished anything she started. She got bored too quickly. It was strange how contented she felt today, just sitting here with Dirk. Normally she could not be still for more than two minutes without getting fidgety, but there was a quietness and a strength in Dirk that seemed to calm her restlessness. He seemed so much older and wiser than other boys his age. Perhaps the terrible experiences he had been through had something to do with it, or perhaps she herself had changed.

She leaned back against the wall of the little fort, stretching her legs out before her, and watched the breeze ruffle Dirk's hair as he bent over the shoe he was carving. "What made you decide to join the East India Company, Dirk?" she asked idly.

"I didn't," he said, looking up. "My family decided for me."

"Did you mind?"

He shrugged. "There wasn't much point. Besides, I had to leave home; I'd become somewhat of an embarrassment there."

"An embarrassment? You? How could anyone possibly find you an embarrassment?"

Dirk put down his work and brushed the wood shavings from his lap. His brown eyes smiled at her mildly. "I'm a bastard," he said, "the result of my father's indiscretion with the family maid when he was no older than I am now. The poor girl died in childbirth so his family kept me and brought me up in their household."

"How very noble of them," said Julie acidly. Dirk shrugged.

"I can't complain, they treated me well enough and, after all, they could easily have disowned me and had me sent to a God-house. That's a home for children with no parents," he explained, as he saw Julie's puzzlement. "Anyway, all went well for some time, but two years ago my father decided to marry and that was when I became an embarrassment. You see, he had never officially acknowledged me but, as I grew older, I had become uncomfortably like him in appearance. My grandparents decided the most prudent thing would be to get me out of the house before his bride saw me, so they paid their bond to the Company and had me apprenticed as a ship's carpenter."

"But that's terrible," said Julie.

"It's life. Don't things like that happen where you . . . in your time?"

"Oh, no," she said, but then she thought of some of the children she knew, who had been virtually kicked out of home by uncaring parents. "Yes," she conceded. "I guess we haven't really become any nicer."

"Tell me about your world," he asked her.

She shook her head. "It's too complicated. I'd rather talk about you. Is it a good life, at sea?"

"It's hard," he said. "It can be very bad. It depends on your officers. Jacobz was one of the worst. I've seen men flogged half to death by him when he was in one of his drunken rages. The Commandeur was better; strict, but always just. Jacobz hated him."

"Is that what sparked the mutiny plot?"

"Partly. They had a flaming row while we were anchored at the Cape of Good Hope. Jacobz and his doxy had been all round the fleet on a drinking binge and when he came back on board Pelsaert really let fly at him. He told him he was a disgrace to his country and his profession and that if he didn't mend his ways he'd have him relieved of his command."

"I bet that went down well."

"It did. It's my belief Jacobz would have killed him there and then if there hadn't been so many other ships around. As it was he contrived to lose the rest of the fleet soon after we left the Cape and he and Jan Evertz and some of the others hatched this plot to incite a mutiny."

"Go on. What did they do?"

"Well, there was this woman on board; Lucretia Jansz. Jacobz had set his cap at her but she turned him down. Rumour has it she fancied the Commandeur, but I think it was only gossip: she had a husband in Batavia. Anyway, one night some of the men seized her and stripped her and plastered her with tar. There was the devil to pay over it. Pelsaert ordered an inquiry and swore to put the culprits in irons and have them tried as soon as we reached Batavia. Of course nobody ever confessed but it was an open secret that Jan Evertz had been the ringleader and Jacobz had incited him to do it. Jacobz intended to use Evertz's arrest as an excuse to start his mutiny, but in the meantime, of course, he ran the ship aground and that was the end of that. Both he and Evertz will have some fast talking to do in Batavia if they want to save their necks."

"And where does Jeronimus Cornelisz fit into all this?"

"Cornelisz? Who can tell? He is a man who keeps his

own counsel; but he certainly used the situation for his own ends. I told you he was a follower of Torrentius."

"But who is Torrentius?"

Dirk looked amazed. "Torrentius van der Beeke; surely you've heard of him?"

She shook her head.

"Torrentius is a heretic."

"My, my," she teased, amused by his shocked tone, "just like you?"

Dirk's brown eyes widened indignantly. "Don't jest about it. This man is evil; wicked. He teaches that there is no devil and no hell."

"So?" Julie failed to see anything so very terrible in that.

Dirk explained. "He teaches that there is no such thing as sin. All thoughts and desires come from God, he says, and since God is all goodness then the desires he puts into our minds must also be good and should therefore be gratified."

"You're joking."

"No, it's true. Aris Jansz was telling me last night what life is like on *Batavia*'s Graveyard. He says Cornelisz and his men strut about like kings. They have seized the Company's chests and dress themselves in looted finery, they kill for no better reason than to pass the time away, and they use the women as harlots. Conraet van Huyssen has taken the predikant's daughter and Jeronimus has Lucretia Jansz; the rest are shared by anyone who wants them."

Julie felt sick. The whole concept seemed too nightmarish to be real, but she remembered the men who had come to Seals Island. She remembered the way they had taunted their terrified captives; their brutal treatment of

Dirk; how they had laughed as he fought for his life and was overpowered and thrown into the sea to drown. No, this was no nightmare. It was cold reality. She looked with new eyes around the comfortless haven of Soldiers Island and breathed a sigh of gratitude for its defenders, and the blunt, honest man who commanded them.

Dirk had finished his clogs. He stood up and slipped his feet into them, walking up and down like a buyer in a shoe shop, testing them for fit. A couple of times he took them off to make minor adjustments, but at last he was satisfied. He grinned at Julie, shuffled his feet experimentally, and broke into a little jig, his wooden soles clattering rhythmically on the flat limestone. Julie laughed. She egged him on, clapping her hands in time to the sound and, after a moment, a couple of soldiers joined in. One of them produced a little home-made fife. Dirk danced across to Julie and made her an elaborate bow. She gave him her hand and, pulling her to her feet, he began to whirl her round to the music — faster and faster until she was quite giddy and out of breath. The soldiers clapped and whistled and some of them began to sing in French. Before long the whole camp had gathered to watch them. They cheered and stamped and the noise they made was so great that the lookout, running up from the beach, had to shout to make himself heard above the din.

"They're coming!" he yelled. "Cornelisz's men. They're coming to attack us!"

9

THE MUSIC STOPPED: cut dead. Its echoes haunted an apprehensive silence. The defenders glanced almost furtively at one another, and on their faces could be read the same questions. Are we prepared? Are we strong enough? Can we hold them? Suddenly, as if on a spoken command, they snatched up weapons and began to run towards the beach. Dirk and Julie ran with them, caught up in the air of urgency. On the small cliffs overlooking the bay they stopped and stood silently, gazing out across the shallows, where two boats bobbed up and down on a slight swell. Julie counted the occupants; around twenty as far as she could make out. She strained her eyes, trying to pick out individual faces. As she watched, one of the men leapt out and began to splash his way towards the shore. She felt Dirk's fingers close around her arm.

"It's Pietersz," he hissed, "Jacop Pietersz; the bastard who tried to drown me."

"Who are the others? Is Cornelisz there?"

"I don't see him." Dirk's voice shook with fury as he

watched the man who had tried to murder him. "By God, if that bilge rat sets foot on this island I'll tear him apart." He snatched up a rock and would have hurled it, but Hayes stopped him.

"Don't waste your ammunition, boy. Wait till they show their hand."

Ranged along the rocks, the defenders stood motionless as Pietersz approached. No-one spoke. Suddenly he stopped and raised his arms in a gesture of goodwill. "We come in peace," he shouted. "We mean you no harm."

Hayes cupped his hands to his mouth. "It won't work, Pietersz; I know you too well. You couldn't lie straight in a coffin!"

Pietersz took a couple more steps and stopped again. "I mean it. I only want to talk to you."

"So, talk. I can hear you."

"Let me come ashore first."

Hayes picked up a stone and began to toss it from hand to hand. "You think I'm a fool? You set one foot on this beach and I'll smash your head in."

"Don't push us, Hayes. We can take this pathetic little island of yours any time we want."

"Come and try then." Hayes closed his fist around the rock he was juggling and flung it out across the water. It dropped almost at Pietersz's feet, splashing him with spray. He let out a bellow of rage and, ripping his cutlass from his belt, charged for the beach like an angry bull, followed by his cohorts, who had closed in behind him while he was talking.

Despite their rage, they were clumsy in the shallow water, slipping and stumbling on the rocks and mud. Hayes waited until they were within range; then he shouted "Now!", and their curses turned to howls of outraged pain as a hailstorm of coral stones hammered about their shoulders. The ferocity of the attack took them by surprise and, though they threatened and cursed and promised all manner of blood-curdling reprisals, they had no answer to the relentless barrage. With stockpiles of ammunition ready to hand, the defenders pressed their attack mercilessly and, step by step, their would-be assailants were driven back towards their boats. Julie, hurling rocks with the best of them, found herself swept away in a storm of violence. She heard her voice bawling obscenities in Dutch and English and her arm swung like a spear-thrower, over and over again, oblivious to strain or exhaustion. A red haze clouded her vision and she was conscious of nothing but the need to fight and keep on fighting. "I got him," screamed Dirk's voice beside her. "I hit the bastard right in the guts!" and she had a fleeting impression of Pietersz, doubled over with pain, staggering back towards his boat. But then the battle-rage swept over her again, and she didn't even realise it was over until Hayes himself caught her arm and took the rock out of her hand.

"Steady, child, steady. It's done. We've driven them off."

Slowly she relaxed. She was shaking all over, her breath was coming in gasps, and she realised she was utterly exhausted. She looked up into Hayes's face. "We did it," she panted. "We did it."

"Yes," he grinned, "we did it; and you no less than any of us. Before God, *kindje*, you fought like a tiger!" With a triumphant shout he scooped her up in his arms and ran down the beach with her to join his men, who had gathered on the shoreline to hurl insults at their retreating foe. Dirk capered around them, cheering wildly.

Once out of range the mutineers regained a little of their bravado. Pietersz turned and shook his fist defiantly. "You've just signed your own death warrants Hayes. The Captain General will have you flayed alive for this, all of you."

Jeers and catcalls were his only answer:

"Let's see him catch us first!"

"Cornelisz couldn't take the skin off an egg custard; he's nothing but a bag of wind!"

Only Hayes remained thoughtful and when at last the boats had drawn beyond shouting range, and the defenders swaggered triumphantly back to their camp, he spoke to them seriously. "Don't get over-confident," he warned them. "We haven't won a war, only a skirmish — and a fairly minor one at that."

"You think they'll be back, then?" asked Dirk.

Hayes fixed him with a keen, blue gaze. "Son, there is nothing in this world more certain. The only question is how soon."

They were given barely a week. Nine days after the first attack a lookout rushed into the camp to say that the mutineers were approaching the beach again and that this time they had three boats. Once more the defenders trooped down to the bay to stand by their replenished piles of ammunition and await the arrival of their foe.

"Well, well, look who they've brought with them," jeered Jan Carstensz, pointing to a scarlet-clad figure in the first boat. Julie followed his gaze. She turned to Dirk.

"Cornelisz," he affirmed.

"I've seen him before," said Julie, shuddering as she remembered. "He was watching from the beach on Bea... on *Batavia*'s Graveyard, the day they came for you and Jan." She stared, mesmerised, at the flamboyant figure, instigator of so much horror and bloodshed. Dirk said nothing, but his hand tightened around the stone he was holding; his face, white and taut beneath its fading bruises, was set in a mask of grim determination. Clearly, he had a score to settle.

As they watched, Cornelisz's boat pulled in to a rocky islet opposite the bay. Several of the rowers jumped out and held it steady while... "My God, they've got women with them," exclaimed Hayes, staring as though he could not believe his eyes, as five long-skirted figures were handed ashore.

It was true. The women stood together on the shore as the boat pulled out again, a forlorn little group in their looted finery. Even at that distance their faces looked unnaturally pale and it was pathetically obvious that none of them was there by choice.

"Poor little bitches," murmured Hayes. Then his voice rose sharply. "I see our illustrious undermerchant does not intend to get his fancy shoes wet either. Look!" and he pointed. Cornelisz had remained behind with his captive harem. Someone had brought a wine barrel ashore and on this he sat in splendour, like a king at a tournament, anticipating the coming carnage.

"Gutless bastard," spat Jan Carstensz. His eyes flickered across the little group and suddenly his voice broke in an agonised cry: "Anneken! My God, they've got Anneken!" Snatching a pike from the man next to him, he rushed down the beach and would have flung himself single-handed onto the attackers if his comrades had not stopped him. Ignoring his curses, they dragged him back to safety, but even then one of them had to hit him hard across the face before he came to his senses and collapsed, sobbing, on the beach. From the water, the mutineers laughed mockingly.

"What's the matter Jan? Aren't you pleased to see your pretty little wife? We dote on her; would you like us to strip her off and show you how much we love her?"

"Get him out of here," ordered Hayes as Carstensz began to roar and struggle again. Two of his mates overpowered the grief-crazed man and dragged him back to the fort.

"They'll pay for it, Jan," Hayes promised fiercely. "Sooner or later we'll make them pay the price."

"It looks as if they mean business this time," muttered one of the soldiers uneasily, as the marauders splashed their way purposefully towards the shore. "Look at those pikes!"

Hayes scanned the opposition with anxious eyes. "Never mind the pikes; they'll have to get a lot closer before they can use them. Can you see any muskets?"

Muskets! Julie started in horror. It had never crossed her mind that they might have guns. She scoured the advancing ranks but, to her relief, could see nothing that resembled firearms.

"I can't understand it," Hayes was muttering. "They have all our guns and ammunition. Why don't they use them?"

"Perhaps..." Before Dirk could finish, the enemy was within range and, with a roar, the defenders launched their attack.

The battle raged for what seemed like hours, though

in truth it cannot have been more than thirty minutes or so. The mutineers were better prepared this time, and more determined. They had made crude shields to protect themselves from the rocks and spread out widely to present a less concentrated target. Even so, they could make little headway against the steady bombardment from the shore. The defenders, too, had learnt valuable lessons from their first encounter and were putting them to good use. A few of the marauders did eventually get close enough to come to grips with their assailants, but they were grossly outnumbered and soon driven back by a hedge of home-made pikes.

At last it was all over and once again Hayes had emerged victorious. As the mutineers retreated across the shallows he and his men pursued them desperately, trying to reach Cornelisz and the women before they could be taken off the island. It was a valiant effort but the distance was just too great. In the end they could only watch in helpless frustration as the boats pulled off in the direction of *Batavia*'s Graveyard.

It was a rather subdued little group that returned to the camp to celebrate their victory. Nobody felt very triumphant. Jan Carstensz sat with his head in his hands, refusing all efforts to console him, and some of the more hot-headed among his friends had to be restrained from wreaking their vengeance on Daniel Cornelissen. Squabbles flared between the French and Dutch factions and everyone was irritable and out of sorts. Obviously, they had all had enough: they were cold, they were uncomfortable, and they had been penned up on this island for over six weeks now, thirsting for vengeance and frustrated by their inability to carry the fight to their enemy. The prospect of rescue, which had kept them going for so long, now seemed nothing more than a cruel illusion. The world around them was a wasteland of treacherous water and the ceaseless, soulless, mind-destroying Abrolhos wind was slowly sapping their very sanity. One or two of them began to question the wisdom of prolonging the struggle and pressed Hayes to seek a truce with Cornelisz.

Hayes rebuffed them vigorously. "Have you forgotten the treachery that left us stranded here?" he asked them. "Or the things that have been done on the other islands?" Dirk and Aris Jansz supported him, reaffirming their own experiences, but in the emotion-charged atmosphere their words met with a mixed response. To those who had not witnessed it, the very horror of the stories made them seem barely credible. People remembered Cornelisz's letter and began to question whether the stories might not be exaggerations. By evening tempers were running hot, and it was a disturbed and sharply divided camp that finally settled down for the night.

Julie found sleep impossible. She lay awake in her little corner of the fort, staring up at the stars through gaps in the sealskin roof. The arguing disturbed her. The relief of finding shelter and protection was already starting to wear off and she was feeling lonely and homesick. Was she really doomed to spend the rest of her life on this godforsaken island? And suppose rescue did come — what then? For the others, even Dirk, there were homes and families waiting, but what would happen to her once they reached Batavia? She wanted desperately to talk to Dirk, but when she looked across at him he was asleep, curled up like a child beneath his rugs, his face pale and strangely beautiful in the moonlight. She hadn't the heart to wake him. Beside him Jean Reynouw, one of the French soldiers, was also awake. He was propped on one elbow, watching her: when he saw her looking at him he grinned and blew her a kiss. She turned away, but a chill crept into her heart. There had been an unmistakable invitation in that gesture: it was a danger she had not thought of before.

By next day heads had cooled a little but the differences were still far from being resolved. Everyone had his own theory on what should be done and a few of the French soldiers even began to talk of taking the little boat and visiting Cornelisz under a flag of truce. Hayes decided the best way to keep the various factions from each other's throats was to keep them busy. He set groups of men to work replenishing the supplies of ammunition. Those with wood and metal-working skills continued making weapons, and a group was sent across in the boat to High Island to search for flotsam and driftwood. "Keep your eyes open," Hayes warned them. "One of Cornelisz's boats called in there yesterday. See if you can find out what they were up to."

Their only boat, the little makeshift skiff in which Aris Jansz had escaped from *Batavia*'s Graveyard, was kept on a beach on the northern shore. The beach was not visible from the camp and Julie, out hunting for birds' eggs, was the first to spot the expedition returning from East Wallabi. She watched the men drag their little vessel onto the sand and saw them lift from it something wrapped in a piece of canvas. From the shape she guessed it to be piece of timber, perhaps a portion of one of the masts. Whatever it was, it was apparently no ordinary find for, with great care, two of the men hefted it onto their shoulders and a silent, almost ceremonial, procession followed it back to the fort. Julie trailed along in the rear, full of curiosity but reluctant to ask questions. There was something in the bearing of the men that discouraged chatter.

At last they reached the camp. As they came in people glanced up from their work, curious, as Julie had been, and surprised to see the party back so soon. None of the men spoke and not until they had a large audience around them did the bearers finally lay their burden down on the flat limestone. Claas Jansz pulled back the canvas. A gasp of disbelieving horror escaped from a score of throats; Hayes swore violently; Julie's belly cramped with revulsion and she fought back an overwhelming need to vomit. It was a man, or what was left of him — the crabs and gulls had been busy during the night; but it was neither crabs nor gulls that had inflicted on him the injuries from which he had died. His head had been battered to a pulpy mess, intestines oozed from a gaping hole in his belly and his right arm, hacked through at the shoulder and attached by only a few shreds of flesh and sinews, dangled grotesquely, like the limb of a discarded marionette.

The whole camp looked down at him and then at one another. Nobody spoke; there was no word in any language that would have been adequate. Finally Hayes broke the silence. "Does anyone know who he is?"

They shook their heads. Jan Carstensz stooped and studied the face, but the features were so mutilated as to be unrecognisable. "Could be almost anyone," he pronounced. "From the clothes I'd say an officer, but of course they may not be his own. Cornelisz has been very free with all the sea-chests."

Aris Jansz, who had arrived late, shouldered his way

through the crowd and stood staring down at the battered corpse. For a moment he hesitated, then, dropping to his knees, he took one stiff hand in his own and turned it over slowly. His fingers traced the line of a thin, white scar across the palm. When he looked up there were tears in his eyes and his whole face was twisted with grief. "It's the surgeon-barber," he said.

"Maistre Franz!" The name was passed back and forth in shocked whispers among the crowd. "Are you certain, Aris?"

"Of course I'm certain." The young man was weeping openly now. "I worked with the man for eight months. He was my master. How would I not know him?" He lifted distraught eyes to Hayes. "*Why,* Weibbe? Why would they do this to him? He hadn't harmed them."

Hayes hunched his shoulders and let them fall again helplessly. "Who knows? For spite, for pleasure, for revenge; do they need a reason any longer?"

Dirk said: "He would not kill for them. They sent him twice to Seals Island and both times he sat in the boat and would not go ashore. Perhaps they were afraid he would come over to us."

Weibbe Hayes lifted his head and swept a glance around his silent audience. "Well," he asked bitterly, "do any of you still want to make peace with Jeronimus Cornelisz?"

With all the dignity and ritual they could afford him, Franz Jansz, surgeon-barber of the *Batavia*, was laid to rest among the mutton-bird holes on Soldiers Island. They had no wood to spare for a coffin but they wrapped his body lovingly in a canvas shroud. Weibbe Hayes read the prayers over his grave and Aris Jansz spoke his eulogy, tears coursing unashamedly down his face as he recalled the gentle man who had been his master and his friend. But Maistre Franz's death had not been utterly in vain, for in that lonely grave died all argument in favour of a truce with the mutineers. Suddenly the horror that had been haunting them all these weeks was no longer merely hearsay. It had come among them; they had looked upon it with their own eyes and they understood. There could be no surrender, and no hope of mercy in defeat.

10

AYES HAD warned them to expect another attack almost immediately, but the days went by with no sign of a boat. The horror of Maistre Franz's death gradually receded into an unpleasant memory and spirits began to revive. Some of the soldiers started to get cocky.

"We've got them scared," jeered Jean Reynouw. "We've beaten them twice and they know they're out-numbered. They won't be back in a hurry."

Hayes didn't share the Frenchman's confidence. He continued to post lookouts on the beach and to set a guard on the camp at night. What worried him most was the thought of all those guns left behind on *Batavia*'s Graveyard. "I can't think why Cornelisz doesn't use them," he said, as they sat round their campfire eating supper after yet another uneventful day. "We may outnumber him but we'd be helpless against firearms. What is he playing at?"

"I think I can guess," said Dirk. "I'll wager he's waiting for a ship."

"What do you mean?"

"Well, it stands to reason. Whatever happens to Pelsaert, eventually someone is going to come looking for us and, once they find us, Cornelisz and his cronies are dead meat. So, what would you do in their shoes? They had already planned to run off with the *Batavia*; why not steal the rescue ship instead?"

"But would that be possible?" asked Julie. "Surely the ship would be armed?"

"Armed, but unsuspecting," said Dirk, and Aris Jansz added bitterly, "Aye, and grossly undermanned. Don't forget they'd be expecting to bring back around two hundred survivors. They wouldn't have room for a large crew."

There was a buzz of discussion as the camp pondered this theory.

"It makes sense," agreed Hayes at last. "And if Cornelisz was planning to take the ship he wouldn't want to waste good powder and shot on us." He sighed. "I'd give a lot to know just what's going on in that evil mind of his."

"There's one way to find out," said Jean Reynouw bluntly.

Hayes looked at him and, after a long pause, said: "You're right, Jean. Bring him here. It's time we had a long talk with Mijnheer Cornelissen."

Daniel Cornelissen had been their prisoner for two weeks now, bound hand and foot and untied for only the briefest intervals to eat and relieve himself. His health had suffered and there was little of the swaggering mutineer about him when Jean Reynouw dragged him into the camp. Nevertheless, rather to everyone's surprise, he had retained enough of his arrogance to spit into Hayes's face when the big soldier questioned him about Cornelisz's plans. Anyone else would have struck him. Hayes wiped the spittle away with calm dignity, and when he spoke there was genuine regret in his voice, for, despite his calling, he was not a man of violence.

"Very well, Daniel, you leave me no other choice. Under the circumstances I do not think anyone will deny me the legal right. Aris, fetch me some rope and a piece of canvas."

The young barber hurried off to do his bidding. Cursing and struggling, Cornelissen was pushed to his knees and forced back onto his haunches. His wrists were bound to his ankles and two of the burliest soldiers held him tightly by the shoulders. When he had been completely immobilised, Hayes tied the canvas round his neck so that it stood up about his face like a bucket.

Julie watched in horrified fascination. "What are they going to do to him?" she whispered to Dirk.

"Torture him. They'll fill the canvas with water till he has to swallow it to stop himself from drowning, and as fast as he swallows, they'll keep filling it up. In the end, unless he agrees to talk, he'll either burst or choke."

"But that's barbaric!" protested Julie.

"No more so than the crimes he has committed. And the law allows it under certain circumstances. Anyway, I don't think you need worry. Daniel Cornelissen is not of the stuff of which heroes are made. I doubt whether he'll suffer for very long before he agrees to talk."

Dirk was right. The first time Hayes allowed Cornelissen time to draw breath, the young man begged for mercy and promised he would tell them anything they wished to know if they would only release him. They untied him and took the canvas from round his neck.

"Talk," said Hayes.

As the words came tumbling out in a torrent of information, Dirk's suspicions were soon confirmed: Cornelisz was indeed planning to steal the rescue ship and for this reason was reluctant to use his ammunition. Cornelissen's visit, he confessed, had been for the express purpose of sowing dissent among the French soldiers. If the Captain General could not gain his ends by force then he would do so by guile.

"And what will he try now — now that he sees we are too strong for him?" asked Hayes. Cornelissen did not know. Despite all their threats there was nothing more he could tell them, except to confirm what they themselves were already beginning to realise: that Jeronimus Cornelisz could not afford to leave them alive. "Dead men tell no tales," repeated Cornelissen miserably. "Nor can they carry a warning to would-be rescuers."

It was enough to convince even the most optimistic. There were no more complaints about guard duty or pike drill. Even Julie learnt how to handle the long roughly-made spears. She swung the clubs too, the fearsome hand-carved staves with their bulbous heads inset with nails and iron spikes. Of all the weapons made by the defenders these were surely the most lethal. The soldiers called them 'morning stars', an absurdly beautiful name for such fearsome instruments. Julie could never see them without recalling the ogres in the story books of her childhood, and when she remembered the injuries they had inflicted upon Franz Jansz it made her blood run cold. *'Fee fie fo fum. I smell the blood of an English-man.'* She had nightmares about them sometimes.

Little by little she was settling into her role as a seventeenth century soldier's daughter. It was not as difficult as she had expected it to be. The antiquated Dutch was becoming familiar from constant use and if she had problems she took them to Dirk. Any awkward questions from others she parried by pleading amnesia. She was surprised how easily they had all accepted Dirk's story — to her it seemed patently implausible — but of course they had no reason to question her identity, while her lack of recollection, at least, was completely genuine. Hayes and his soldiers were wonderfully patient with her, trying all manner of devices to jog her memory and filling her in on the 'forgotten' details of her past. Jean Jeynouw offered to re-educate her in her mother tongue but she declined his offer, saying she was sure it would all come back in time. Since that night she had caught him watching her she had been very cautious of the young Frenchman and avoided any situations that might have left her alone in his company. Amongst a hard-living, hard-loving band of soldiers he was noticeably crude and he and Jan Carstensz had already come to blows following bawdy comments concerning their lack of women and the home comforts enjoyed by the mutineers.

Apart from Dirk, Julie's closest companions were Weibbe Hayes and Aris Jansz, the young assistant barber. Hayes was an extraordinary man, blunt, honest and uncomplicated, with the strength and dependability of a rock. A big man in every sense of the word, he had the gentleness that so often goes hand in hand with strength and created about himself an atmosphere of confidence and security. Julie loved him. He treated her with the affection of a favourite uncle and enthralled her with his tales of battle and high adventure. He was in his mid-thirties and had been a mercenary for as long as he cared to remember. Aris was a quiet young man, a couple of years older than Dirk. He had only recently joined the Dutch East India Company and this had been his first voyage. Better educated than most of his companions, he took a keen interest in politics and it was from him that Julie chiefly learnt what was going on in the strange world into which she had fallen.

Charles I had been King of England for three years when the *Batavia* sailed from Holland, and Prince Frederick Henry had recently succeeded his brother Maurice as Stadtholder of the United Netherlands. Julie quickly learnt that Holland was in fact only one of a group of provinces which had fought a long and bitter war of rebellion to obtain their independence from Spain. A truce, signed in 1609, had expired in 1621, just eight years ago, and since then the two countries were snapping at each other's throats again. The Dutch East India Company was engaged in a trade war with England and Portugal; the whole Western World was still wading through the aftermath of the Reformation; and in Germany just about every European nation was dipping spoons into a seething broth that would go down in history as the Thirty Years' War.

Religion seemed to be the burning topic of the day and even on this miserable speck of land at the end of the world heated arguments could develop over issues which seemed to Julie absurdly trivial. Aris was a devout Calvinist and embroiled himself in frequent and passionate debates with the French soldiers, both parties equally convinced that the other was irrevocably doomed to hell. Dirk, as a result of his affection for the Catholic Annetje, was more broad-minded. In this matter he had the support of Weibbe Hayes. Hayes, the soldier of fortune, had seen too many good men killed in the name of religion and felt there were things more worth dying for than the doctrines of predestination or the infallibility of the Pope. "I sometimes think," he would say, in his blunt Dutch fashion, "that the Lord God must weep tears of blood when he sees what we have done with the faith he gave us." Julie had to agree with him. She tried to console herself with the thought that her own generation seemed much wiser in this respect, but when she reflected on the struggles going on in her world she had to admit that some things had not really improved much in three hundred years.

The days dragged into weeks until almost a month had passed and still there was no sign of the mutineers. There was much speculation as to what might be happening on *Batavia*'s Graveyard. Was Cornelisz preparing another expedition? Was he building boats or making more weapons? Could it be that, having disposed of their opposition, the mutineers had begun to fall out among themselves? All sorts of wild suggestions were made. Jan Carstensz and the trumpeter, Claas Jansz, whose wife was also a captive on *Batavia*'s Graveyard, begged to be allowed to take the boat and sneak over there one night to rescue them. Hayes denied their request, reasonably enough, for it would have been an extremely foolhardy enterprise; but his refusal caused another upsurge of bad feeling, and tempers began to fray again.

When at last two of the mutineers' yawls were spotted approaching the island the news was received almost with relief. Weapons were gathered and once more the little company prepared to defend itself. It seemed however that Cornelisz was in no hurry to attack. Before the astonished eyes of the onlookers he landed his men on the islet opposite the bay and proceeded to set up camp. He had brought the women with him again and someone else also, a man Julie had not seen before; his lugubrious, black-clad figure stuck out like a grim omen amid the peacock finery of the mutineers. His presence provoked ribald laughter among the defenders. They cupped their hands to their mouths and bellowed across the water: "What are you trying to do, Cornelisz, *pray us to death?*"

"You must be desperate if you've got to bring the predikant to fight for you!"

"Look after him well, you villains; you're going to need him. After we've finished with you he can bury you!"

Cornelisz ignored the jeers. When he had completed his preparations he and two of his companions boarded the smaller of the boats and began to row towards the edge of the shallows. One of the men was holding up a piece of white cloth tied to the end of a stick.

Hayes watched them through narrowed eyes. "That's far enough," he shouted at last. "You can speak your piece from there."

Cornelisz made a sign to the rowers and they shipped their oars. He stood up and cupped his hands to his mouth. "We want to talk to you."

"I'm listening."

"Be reasonable, Hayes; I can't shout from here."

"Suit yourself; you're not getting any closer."

"We want to make a truce with you."

Hayes thought about this for a moment. "State your terms then and I'll consider them."

Cornelisz opened his mouth to speak but at that moment a wave rocked the little boat. He lost his balance and sat down heavily. Hayes's men roared with laughter.

"This is ridiculous, Hayes. We can't have a proper discussion like this."

"Why not?" yelled back Hayes. "I'm quite comfortable."

This was greeted by another howl of mirth. Cornelisz swore. He went into conference with his men and suddenly Julie saw the glint of metal.

"Guns!" she screamed. "They've got guns!"

As one man the defenders threw themselves to the ground. There was a long, nerve-tingling silence. Then Hayes began to laugh. "It helps if your powder is dry," he jeered and Julie, raising a cautious head, saw the muskets dangling uselessly from the hands of two very foolish-looking would-be assassins.

"Next time, find somebody who knows a bit more about guns to do your dirty work," yelled Aris Jansz. The rest of the company hooted derisively.

The abortive attempt at treachery brought negotiations to an abrupt end. Hayes led his men down onto the beach in force and Cornelisz, deciding that discretion was the better part of valour, gave the order to retire. Followed by the whistles and catcalls of the watching soldiers, he was rowed back to the safety of the islet.

The defenders sat down to wait, wondering what the next move would be. The mutineers appeared to be arguing. There was much toing and froing and gathering into agitated groups, accompanied by nodding of heads and excited waving of arms. Finally some action seemed to have been resolved upon. Cornelisz disappeared into one of the tents with the predikant and when they emerged again Bastiensz was holding what appeared to be a letter. He spoke to a couple of the men on the beach and soon the little boat was heading back towards Soldiers Island.

When they had come as close as they dared, Bastiensz climbed out and, clutching his letter in one scrawny, upraised hand, stood awaiting instructions from Hayes. Awkward and frightened, shivering as the icy water lapped around his knees and the wind fluttered the tattered remnants of his coat, he looked like a gaunt, black heron. Hayes shook his head. "My God," he said, "the poor preacher looks half-starved. Heaven knows I never liked him much but I wouldn't have wished this on him." He shouted: "You may come ashore, Maistre Gyjsbert; nobody will do you any harm." To the men nearest him he said: "Otto, Marcus, go and help the predikant."

Obediently, the two men waded out through the shallows and brought the shivering Gyjsbert Bastiensz back to the beach. Close up he presented a pitiful figure. His tall, thin frame was stooped with exhaustion, his hands wizened into fleshless claws, while his haggard, ghost-ridden face was little more than a death's head, dominated by cavernous eyes and a huge, beaked nose. When Hayes clasped him about the shoulders in a compassionate embrace he began to cry, loudly and horribly. He fell to his knees and wrapped his arms about the soldier's legs, clinging to him like a child. "Don't send me back," he begged. "For the love of God, don't make me go back to them. They want to kill me."

Very gently, Hayes prised open the clutching hands and lifted him back to his feet. "Have no fear Maistre Gyjsbert; you're safe with us. No-one will make you go back again. Now, come to our fort and let me give you something to eat; then we will discuss the terms Jeronimus wishes to offer."

Bastiensz went meekly, still clinging to the big friendly arm that supported him. Hayes's sympathetic reception seemed to have opened a floodgate on his misery and his voice stumbled as frequently as his legs as he poured out into this first sympathetic ear an incoherent tale of woe. "All of them," Julie heard him mumbling as they disappeared along the well-worn track leading back to the fort, "... all of them ... in one night ... even the baby. I thought I would go mad."

Once they had left there was nothing for the rest of them to do but wait, and keep a watch on Cornelisz and his cronies. Julie sat down beside Dirk. "So that's the man who wanted to have you flogged," she said. "He doesn't look very intimidating now, does he?"

"Poor bastard," said Dirk.

She stared at him indignantly. "Poor bastard nothing! It serves him right! What's the matter with you, Dirk, don't you ever hate anyone?"

Dirk laughed. "Proper little hell-cat aren't you? Nobody would ever cross you and get away with it."

"Why should they?" she demanded.

He shook his head and there was a note of sadness in his voice. "Life's too short to hold grievances. That's one lesson I've learnt over these past months. Besides, no-one could deserve what he's been through. Did you know they murdered his whole family?"

"What?"

"Yes, his wife and six children, all in one night. They invited the old man and his eldest daughter to a meal and then went to his tent and butchered all the others; beat their brains in with adzes and buried them in a pit."

"How do you know?"

"Aris told me. That's why they tried to kill him: because he saw what was going on."

"Dear God!" Julie's brain reeled as she tried to picture the scene. It was almost beyond comprehension. She asked in a small voice, "How old were they, Dirk?"

"Children," he said harshly, "except the eldest son. The youngest was a little boy called Roelant. He was just two."

Two years old! In her mind's eye Julie pictured the tiny body with its head crushed in like that of the surgeon-barber's. She began to cry. "When will it stop?" she sobbed. "Oh, Dirk, when will it all be over? I can't take it any longer. I don't belong here, I want to go home. I want my Dad."

The last sentence came out as the wail of a lost child. Dirk took her into his arms and rocked her gently. "Oh, Julie, don't cry, don't be frightened, I'll look after you. You saved my life once; don't let go now. I need you. I love you."

Through her tears she blinked at him in bewilderment. The words jangled in her mind. How often and how lightly had they been said to her before? How casually had she tossed them off herself? They were the currency of her generation, the gambling chips of teen-age relationships: 'I love you — don't give me a hard time. I love you — don't hassle me.' But this was different. Dirk's 'I love you' had none of these connotations; despite his worldly wiseness he was probably the most unsophisticated sixteen-year-old she had ever met. When he said 'I love you' he meant just that — no conditions, no demands. His love was totally innocent. And yet there was nothing childish about it. It made her

114

feel a woman far more than the leering overtures of Jean Reynouw had done. She remembered what her father had said: '*If you would be loved then first you must love and be lovable*'. Was she lovable? It was not a term she would have applied to herself. In her experience, staying on top of the heap was what counted and that meant being the toughest and the smartest. To love was to be vulnerable and therefore weak. Yet Dirk said he loved her, and Dirk was certainly not weak.

She moved closer into his arms, feeling their strength around her and the warmth of his breath on her cheek. She relaxed, strangely at peace with herself. Suddenly, to be loved by Dirk seemed the most wonderful thing in the world. Perhaps, she thought, her father had only been half right. Perhaps this thing could work both ways, and knowing that you were loved could in its turn make you loving and lovable. With all her heart she hoped so.

11

WEIBBE HAYES and the predikant were gone for a long time. When at last they returned to the beach, Hayes called his men together. "Jeronimus Cornelisz wishes to make a truce with us," he told them. "He has promised us wine and clothing and canvas to make tents and asks to be allowed to come over and discuss terms."

The defenders looked nervously towards the islet, where the mutineers were awaiting their decision. "Do you think we can trust him?" someone asked.

"Of course not," said Hayes, "but if he comes alone he can't do much harm and if the others try to start anything we'll have him as a hostage. We don't have to agree to any of his demands but I think we should at least find out what they are."

"And it would be nice to have wine again and some decent clothes in place of these stinking hides," added Cornelis Jansz wistfully.

Jan Carstensz said: "What about the women? I'm not agreeing to anything until I get Anneken back."

"That's right," added Claas Jansz emphatically. "You tell that tripe-faced cur we want our wives back before we sign any treaty."

"I'm not suggesting we should sign anything yet," said Hayes patiently, "only that we should hear what he has to say. Now, can we take a vote on it?"

There was a lot of mumbling and grumbling but finally it was agreed that Cornelisz should be given the chance to prove his good faith. "But not tonight," shouted Hayes as he bellowed his invitation across the water. "It will be dark soon and I'm damned if I want you on my island overnight. You can come in the morning."

"Very well," agreed Cornelisz, "but I shall need help to carry all the gear from the boat."

Hayes thought for a moment. "You may bring four men with you," he said at last, "but no more; and if we see even the slightest evidence of weapons . . . " He drew a finger across his throat in a manner that made further words unnecessary.

Cornelisz went into conference with his henchmen. "Very well," he concurred, "but we want a guarantee of your good faith. Put it in writing and send it back with the predikant."

Gyjsbert Bastiensz's face drained of colour and he clutched at Hayes's arm with terrified fingers. "You promised!" he whispered. "You promised!"

Weibbe Hayes patted him reassuringly. "Maistre Gyjsbert is staying here with us," he shouted back to Cornelisz. "He's our predikant too and we haven't had a good sermon in months. You have my word as to our good faith; take it or leave it."

Cornelisz clearly thought little of this arrangement,

but no amount of threatening or cajoling would induce Hayes to change his mind, and in the end he had to agree. The two camps settled down to watch each other through the night. Weibbe Hayes impressed on his little band the need for vigilance. He warned them to be alert for any sign of betrayal. In the back of his mind was the memory of Daniel Cornelissen's treacherous letter and he had no illusions regarding his men. They were mercenaries, soldiers of fortune who fought wherever they were paid to do so. Among such a band, especially when loyalties had already been strained by hardship, bribery and inducement could be powerful weapons.

Next morning everyone was astir early and the whole camp was assembled on the beach when the embassy from *Batavia*'s Graveyard came ashore bearing its gifts. Julie could hardly take her eyes off the Captain General. She had expected some wild, uncouth pirate, but Jeronimus Cornelisz, elegant and supremely self-assured in scarlet coat and golden braid, was almost breathtaking in his splendour. His chestnut hair flowed like a lion's mane about his shoulders, and his beard was brushed and neatly trimmed. He was a big man, almost as big as Weibbe Hayes, and in his shadow Hayes seemed very much the common soldier. Julie could understand now how he had wielded so much influence over the bewildered castaways of *Batavia*'s Graveyard. Even knowing what she did of him, she found it hard to believe he could have been responsible for such atrocities. It was only when she looked deeper into those wide, tawny eyes that she began to understand. There was something untamed in them, an air of suppressed anger that all the outward show could not quite conceal. Julie could feel it in the very air about him — when he smiled at her she moved instinctively closer to Dirk — and she wondered if the others could sense it also.

Before the wondering eyes of the ragged defenders, Cornelisz's companions spread out their gifts, like merchants displaying their wares. There were five men, one more than the four Hayes had stipulated, but this indiscretion was allowed to pass without comment. He examined the sheets of canvas, smiled with satisfaction at the bolts of linen and fine woollen cloth, tasted the cheese — an almost forgotten luxury — and with a great show of good will supervised the broaching of one of the wine casks. Soon the company had broken up into convivial little groups, defenders and mutineers toasting together the success of the forthcoming truce, while the two leaders sat down to discuss terms.

Julie and Dirk found themselves in a group which included Jacop Pietersz and most of the French soldiers. It was not the company either of them would have chosen but Jean Reynouw had insisted, seating Julie beside him, with a proprietary arm around her waist. Rather than cause a scene she had acquiesced, but she was grateful for the reassuring presence of Dirk on her other side. They had been instructed to treat their visitors with courtesy and she wondered how Dirk would manage to control his hatred of Pietersz. Dirk was, however, a master of self-discipline. He greeted the man who had tried to murder him with barely a flicker of emotion.

Pietersz was in an expansive mood. He embraced the soldiers like long lost friends and kissed Julie over-fondly on the mouth. When the wine had been shared out he raised his beaker to her with an elaborate gesture. "To wine and beautiful women," he said, and he winked at Jean Reynouw. "I'm glad to see you have not been entirely starved of female company."

The Frenchman grinned. "We do all right," he said, giving Julie a suggestive squeeze. She would have lashed out at him, but Dirk's hand closed protectively around her own and she relaxed again. Jean wasn't worth it; besides losing her temper would help no-one. One of the other soldiers spoke sharply to Reynouw in French and she realised with some relief that his companions at least knew him to be lying.

Pietersz took a long swig of wine and belched contentedly. "Ah, but on *Batavia*'s Graveyard you could have your pick; you'd think you were in paradise." His face creased into a lecherous smirk. "Zussie Fredericsz: now there's a woman for you; more spirit than a cask of gin. Fought like a tiger, she did, the first few times, but we soon knocked it out of her."

Julie felt sick. Dirk's grip tightened on her hand and she could sense his anger, but she didn't dare to look at him. Pietersz took another gulp of wine. "Drink up, drink up," he urged. "There's plenty more where that came from. Jeronimus looks after his friends."

"So we've heard," said Julie, tartly. She couldn't help it; the words just slipped out. Pietersz laughed. "Don't you worry, dear girl, we'll take very good care of you." He glanced slyly round the little group. "Yes," he said again, "Jeronimus looks after his friends," and he jingled the leather pouch on his belt.

The sound drew all eyes like a magnet and, when he saw he had their undivided attention, he untied the drawstring and poured a stream of gold coins onto the ground. The soldiers stared in awe at the glittering pile.

"And that's only a fraction of it," said Pietersz softly.

"There's six thousand guilders apiece waiting for you on *Batavia*'s Graveyard. More than you could earn in a lifetime."

There was an uneasy silence; the soldiers glanced furtively at one another, each trying to gauge what his companions might be thinking.

"Nice," commented Dirk at last. "How much water will it buy when the rain barrels run out?"

The Lieutenant General turned slowly to consider him. "You should put a bridle on that mouth of yours," he said, and there was a message in his eyes that belied his bantering tone. "A runaway tongue can get you into all sorts of trouble."

"He's right, though," said Thomas de Villier. "Weibbe Hayes is not going to sell his precious water for six thousand guilders."

Pietersz smiled and Julie thought of a cat with a mouse between its paws. "But Weibbe Hayes is not going to be offered six thousand guilders," he said gently.

Nobody spoke. Pietersz's eyes travelled slowly from man to man as he waited for his meaning to sink in; then he continued: "You soldiers are not Dutch; you owe him no loyalty. How many of you would have followed him here if you had been offered the choice? Hayes will never agree to friendship between us. He is power-hungry. He wants to keep this island and the water for himself. Does he treat you fairly? ask yourselves; who are his favourites? Aris Jansz, a thief who stole the boat of his comrades; Cornelis Jansz, who escaped the sentence justly imposed on him by the council and fled here to spread his lies amongst you; Marcus Symonsz and those two scoundrels the Wagenaars brothers — criminals all of them. Hayes encourages them. He listens to their lies and uses them to poison your minds against Jeronimus."

The soldiers muttered uncomfortably. Julie stole a glance round the beach. Everywhere there were little groups with their heads down in earnest conversation. She had a sudden, terrible conviction that they were all discussing the same thing. Hayes, deep in conference with Cornelisz, seemed oblivious to the danger.

"Six thousand guilders," tempted Pietersz again, "for the lives of a few criminals."

Dirk yawned and said loudly: "Your list is as short as your memory, Pietersz. Would you like me to add to it?"

Everyone turned to look at him. The Lieutenant General scowled and gestured to Reynouw to silence the boy, but Dirk had already risen to his feet and was reciting in a voice that carried to every corner of the camp: "Jan Stoffels, fifteen years old, cabin boy, drowned; Mayken Soers, seven months pregnant, battered to death; Bastiaan Gyjsbertsen; Roelant Gyjsbertsen; Frans Fransz — shall I go on?"

Every eye on the island was fixed on him. The soldiers blinked and shook themselves as if awakened from a spell, and Pietersz realised he had lost them. He turned on Dirk a look of pure savagery. "Boy, you have just put your own name on the top of that list. By the time we have finished with you you will wish you had died with your companions."

Dirk ignored him. He turned to where Hayes and Cornelisz had come to their feet, bristling at each other like a pair of bull terriers. He raised his drink. "I give you a toast, Mijnheer Cornelisz. Absent friends!" And he flung the beaker at the Captain General.

It landed well short, but the violence of the gesture ignited a powder-keg of long suppressed frustration. Bellowing with rage, the defenders flung themselves on their treacherous guests. Only Pietersz escaped. With some warning of what was to happen, he had edged far enough away from his group to have a head start, but his companions were quickly beaten to the ground and trussed like turkeys. Cornelisz made one futile grab at his opponent's weapon before being flattened by a single blow from Hayes's ham-like fist. The big soldier stood over him with levelled pike. "Just give me an excuse..." he threatened. But Cornelisz was too stunned to move.

Jacop Pietersz fled for his life through the shallows, with the pack snapping at his heels. "Murder!" he screamed. "Treachery! Help me!"

His companions, watching from their camp, roared with indignation and began to drag their boats into the water. The sun glinted on an arsenal of muskets and cutlasses. Hayes appraised the situation in one swift glance. Leaving others to bind the stunned Cornelisz, he ran down to the shore.

"Get back," he roared to his men. "Get back to your posts; they'll cut you to pieces," and as the soldiers returned hastily to the safety of the shore he turned on the four struggling captives. "*Vermoord ze!*" he ordered. "Kill them; they're too much of a risk."

"But they're helpless," protested Cornelis Jansz. "Their hands are tied; they're..."

"I said 'Kill them'!" roared Hayes. "God's blood, man, we're under attack; there's no time for squeamishness." He snatched a 'morning-star' from the hands of the bewildered youth.

Julie turned away. She had no quarrel with Hayes's justice, but she didn't want to watch it. It was done quickly; there were no cries — just the smack of wood against flesh and bone and it was all over. Only Cornelisz was spared and that from no impulse of mercy. Hayes dragged him down to the waterline, where his companions could see him, and threatened to cut his throat if they did not withdraw. At first they ignored him. They rowed up and down in the channel between the two islands, waving their weapons and shouting abuse. One or two of them started to prime their muskets.

Hayes hauled his prisoner to his knees and jabbed him in the Adam's apple with his knife. "Tell them!" he commanded.

Jeronimus squealed. The man who had brought death to so many others stuttered with terror and squirmed like a maggot in Hayes's grasp, but the soldier's big fist was like an iron clamp in his hair. The knife jabbed again and drew blood.

"Tell them!"

"All right," he moaned. "All right." Raising his voice, he called: "Do as he says. Go back. He means it."

The mutineers stared in silence at the grim tableau on the beach and reluctantly retreated to their islet. They remained there for some time, presumably discussing tactics, but eventually struck camp and departed for *Batavia*'s Graveyard.

The defenders crowed with delight as they watched them go, though Jan Carstensz and Claas Jansz were still agonising over the plight of their wives, and Bastiensz, now that his own hide had been saved, was frantic with worry for his sole remaining daughter. Her protector, Coenraat van Huyssen, had been one of those killed, and the predikant wailed loud and long at the thought of her being thrown to the mercy of the pack. Julie found all this breast-beating a trifle hypocritical — if he was so concerned about her, why had he refused to go back and protect her himself? — but she said nothing. She was beginning to learn that issues were seldom as simple as they appeared.

Jeronimus Cornelisz seemed totally stunned by the turnabout in his fortunes. He lay on the coral where Weibbe Hayes had dropped him, his fancy uniform torn and dirty, and watched with glazed eyes as the soldiers gathered up the gifts he had brought and dragged the bodies of his companions into the scrub for burial. Only when they hauled him to his feet to take him back to the fort did he at last find his tongue again. As they led him away he twisted round to face Hayes. "Don't think you've won, my friend," he snarled. "They'll be back for you, and when they get you you'll wish you'd never been born. There'll be no knife across the throat for you. I'll flay every inch of skin off your body and stake you out on the beach for the crabs."

"You'll have to defeat me first," said his captor pleasantly, "and in your position I wouldn't be wagering too heavily on that."

"No? Take a good look around you, Hayes. How many of these men do you think you can trust? They've heard what we have to offer them; they've seen our gold. How long do you think it will be before ... "

This was too much, even for the placid Hayes. With a swift lunge he seized Cornelisz by the front of his coat and dealt him two stinging blows across the face. "One more word, you filthy, pox-ridden whoremonger and it will be your last! I'll cram your six thousand guilders down your throat and watch you choke on them." He flung the helpless man back to the soldiers. "Get him out of my sight. Put him in the fort and tie him up so he can't move. And if he opens his mouth gag him."

They celebrated that night with the wine and precious tobacco brought by the mutineers. Dirk was the hero of the hour, and so many toasts were drunk to him and with him that by the end of the evening he could hardly stand. Eventually he keeled over where he sat and fell asleep, his drinking vessel still clutched in his hand. Julie tried to wake him but he only snored the louder. She began to feel uneasy. Not all the men here were like Reynouw, but the talk on the beach had made her aware of potential danger, and she had relied on Dirk's protection to ward off any unwanted advances. In his present state he would be no use to anyone. She decided to confide in Weibbe, but his answer was predictable. He laughed loudly and put a fatherly arm about her shoulders. "Don't you worry, *kindje*, anyone who touches you will have me to reckon with." And he opened and closed one huge fist in a most reassuring fashion.

Julie breathed a sigh of relief. She looked down at the snoring Dirk. "I think we had better put him to bed. He doesn't look as though he's going to wake up."

Hayes chuckled. "No, I'm afraid his party is over. He is going to be a very remorseful young man when he wakes up in the morning."

12

I T TOOK DIRK three days to recover from his hangover, and he swore grimly that he would never touch another drink as long as he lived. His sore head and hangdog expression were a source of great amusement to his companions. Even Julie had to smile at his misery. He reminded her of her brother, Paul, the day after his eighteenth birthday party.

Life on the island was much more pleasant now that they had adequate shelter and a few little luxuries such as cheese and tobacco. The soldiers began to fashion clothes for themselves from the bolts of cloth, and Julie found herself much in demand as a seamstress. Dressmaking had never been a hobby of hers, but the castaways were uncritical in their gratitude, and she was thankful now for her mother's enforced lessons. For herself she made a long skirt of scarlet *laken* and a rough linen shirt. It was good to be able to take off her own filthy clothes and give them a thorough wash. When they were dry she folded them and put them away safely. They were her only link with her own time and she had no intention of discarding them.

The capture of Cornelisz had put everyone in jubilant spirits; talk returned to the prospects of rescue. It was now almost three months since Pelsaert had gone off to seek help — time enough for him to have reached Java and returned with a vessel. The question on everyone's lips was: Had he made it? Or had he been murdered by Jacobsz, as the mutineers seemed to believe, and his body thrown to the sharks? Either way, the authorities in Batavia must surely be starting to wonder about them by now. Day and night a fire was kept burning on Soldiers Island to alert a possible rescue craft, while the lookouts posted to keep an eye on *Batavia*'s Graveyard daily scanned the horizon for any glimpse of a sail.

Julie had mixed feelings regarding a possible rescue. The idea of spending the rest of her life on this desolate piece of land held no appeal at all but, on the other hand, what would happen to her if and when the Commandeur returned? Despite Dirk's extravagant promises, a sixteen-year-old apprentice ship's carpenter was in no position to support her, and his family was most unlikely to take her in. And suppose Annetje had relatives waiting to claim her; how long would it be before they discovered she was an impostor?

Somehow she had to get back to her own time. But how? Dirk felt the answer lay on Seals Island, where he had first met her. "When this is all over," he said, "we'll go back there; to the beach where you came ashore in your boat. The secret must lie there somewhere. I'll get you home somehow, Julie, I swear I will."

Strangely, she believed him. Since he had told her he loved her she had begun to see things in him she had not noticed before, and she had absolute faith in him. Had he offered to fly her to the moon she would have been waiting confidently for the spaceship to arrive. In the light of his love she was beginning to see herself differently too. Being loved, she discovered, brought unexpected responsibilities. In Dirk's eyes she was someone special; to betray that belief or to hold it cheaply would be to hurt him immeasurably, and not for anything could she have brought herself to hurt Dirk. Whether her affection for him was love she could not truly say. Certainly it was not the romantic fairy-floss of her teenage novels, nor the excitement of those tentative fumblings in the bike sheds behind the basketball courts, but it was warm and real and infinitely precious. It coloured everything she did and brought a glow back to her anxious features. Even the stolid Hayes noticed the change in her. "Eh, *meisje*, it's good to see the roses back in your cheeks," he told her, and he winked. He was a lot more observant than people guessed.

Life had dropped back into routine for the castaways. Weibbe Hayes continued to worry about another attack, but for the next two weeks the weather was so bad a crossing would have been impossible anyway. The wind swung round to the north and blew a gale, and the rain came down in torrents. When at last it was all over, and a morning dawned that was still and sunny, Julie asked if she might use some of their newly collected rainwater to wash her hair. It was a luxury she had been promising herself for a long time. She had pretty hair. Her brother Paul, when he wanted to tease her, called her carrot-top, but she preferred to describe her hair as auburn. It was long and thick, with a slight natural curl, and at night she put it into braids, so that it rippled down her neck like a waterfall when she brushed it out in the morning.

She had not washed it since leaving *Salamander*, and two months' accumulation of salt and sand had left it dull and lifeless.

The others pitched in to help with great enthusiasm. Amongst the goods brought over by the mutineers had been one precious block of soap, and Weibbe Hayes presented Julie with a chunk of this, wrapped in a piece of muslin. Aris scrubbed out one of the cooking pots so she could have warm water, and Dirk stood by with a jug for rinsing. The rest of the camp gathered round with advice and comments, and she felt as though she were giving a command performance. The luxury of soft, sweet-smelling hair was unbelievable. She tried to persuade Dirk to try it but he just laughed and said he couldn't see the point when he would only look exactly the same again a week later.

One of the soldiers had made her a turtleshell comb, with which she teased out all the tangles. Afterwards she and Dirk went for a walk to allow her hair to dry in the wind. They followed the shoreline, keeping well away from the fort where the prisoners were kept. Julie wanted nothing to do with Jeronimus Cornelisz. There was something overwhelmingly evil about him; even though bound and closely guarded, he still frightened her. It was like having a tethered lion on the island, and she had nightmares occasionally in which he escaped and came looking for her. She confided this fear to Dirk and he teased her about it sometimes, very gently, but she noticed nobody ever volunteered for extra guard duty and that when they came back after their two-hour stints they were invariably edgy and sharp-tempered.

Today, however, not even Jeronimus Cornelisz could blight her happiness. She seemed to walk on air; her hair fluttered about her face like a silken veil, and she felt fresh and free and unencumbered. She sang and swung Dirk's hand as they walked, and by the time they stopped at one of the wells she was quite out of breath. Dirk took off one of his clogs and scooped up some water so they could both have a drink. She giggled. "I've heard of champagne out of slippers," she said, "but this is ridiculous."

"What's champagne?" Dirk wanted to know, but she couldn't think of the Dutch name and had to offer a long explanation. Dirk had never heard of the stuff. "You haven't missed much," she told him. "It's overrated; I'd rather have a Coke any day." And then she remembered he didn't know about Coke either, and she laughed again.

They stretched out lazily, side by side on the warm limestone, and he took off his new jacket to make a pillow. "Tell me about your life," he said. "What is it like, the Southland? Do they have cities there? Are they as big as Amsterdam? What sort of a house do you live in?"

She told him as much as she dared, omitting anything that might sound too incredible. After all, how could you describe cars and jumbo jets to someone who had never even seen a steam engine? "Yes, we have cities," she told him, "much bigger than the Amsterdam you know; but Amsterdam has grown a lot, you would hardly recognise it. We have farms too, bigger than you could imagine, and we sell wheat all over the world."

"Even to my country?" asked Dirk.

"I expect so," said Julie, "or perhaps they get theirs from the Common Market."

"And what's that?"

131

Oh hell, she thought, here we go again. If I ever get back to the twentieth century I'm going to have to do something about my social studies! "It's hard to explain, Dirk; a sort of agricultural co-operative in Europe."

"A co-operative?" Dirk chuckled. "I find that hard to imagine. At the moment every country in Europe is busy trying to cut its neighbour's throat. Don't you have wars in your time?"

"Well, yes, we do, but ... Oh Dirk, do we have to talk about war? I've had enough fighting to last me a lifetime."

He propped himself on one elbow and looked down at her. One hand reached out and brushed a stray lock of hair from her face. "Poor little Julie. This has been terrible for you, hasn't it? And you have been so brave; like a lioness." He leaned down and kissed her gently on the lips. She put her arms around him and hugged him tightly till he collapsed on top of her. Her cheek was resting against his.

"Oh, I love you, Dirk. I do love you."

A sudden laugh shattered the moment. They rolled apart and sat up, flustered and embarrassed. Jean Reynouw was standing only a few feet away, gazing down at them. There was a swagger in his stance and a look on his face that could only be described as a leer. By his side stood a companion and fellow Frenchman, Jean Thiriou. "Well now," he drawled, "just look at our two little lovebirds. What a charming sight."

Julie felt the first pricklings of fear. Dirk put an arm round her shoulder. "*Donder op!* Reynouw. Can't we even go for a walk without you following us and spying on us?"

"Walking, were you?" The Frenchman moved closer, till he was standing almost on top of them. "Well now, that's a new name for it." He winked at Dirk. "Don't worry, lad, we aren't going to spoil your fun; but you mustn't be selfish about it. After all, we're all friends here. Isn't that right, Jean?"

Thiriou grinned widely. "Share and share alike, is what I always say."

"You lay one hand on her," threatened Dirk, "and so help me God, I'll kill you."

Reynouw laughed. He threw back his head and roared like a playful lion. "Big words for a little boy," he said.

With a sudden lunge Reynouw leaned forward and plucked Julie from the boy's embrace. He held her against him with one arm around her waist and with the other hand he began to fondle her, slowly and deliberately, as though challenging Dirk to do something about it. Dirk flew at him but Thiriou moved in and grabbed him from behind. He pinned the boy's hands behind his back and flung one arm about his neck in a headlock. Dirk kicked and squirmed and fought like a maniac but the man was far bigger and stronger than he was. He only laughed and tightened his grip, increasing the pressure on Dirk's throat until he started to choke.

Julie screamed. Reynouw slapped her across the face. "Stop it!" he said. But she could not stop. Hysterical images leapt across her mind. It was Seals Island all over again: Jan and Claas huddled on the beach with knives at their throats, Dirk with his face all battered and bleeding and Jacop Pietersz laughing as he swung his cutlass. She screamed and screamed until Reynouw clapped a hand across her mouth to silence her.

"There, now," he said, when at last she had worn herself out and stood shivering in his arms, "that's much more friendly." He tickled her under the chin. "Now you be a nice little girl for us and Jean won't have to hurt young Dirk." She shuddered and stared helplessly at Dirk, half strangled in the grasp of Jean Thiriou. Reynouw's hand moved slowly down the front of her blouse. He chuckled.

Suddenly there was a crashing in the bushes behind them and the next thing she knew Julie was sprawling on the ground and Reynouw was flat on his back beside her with Weibbe Hayes's huge boot in the middle of his chest. Hayes was red-faced with fury. He turned on Thiriou, who was still holding Dirk. "Let him go," he bellowed. "Let him go or I'll kick this bastard's face in." He jolted Reynouw under the jaw with the toe of his boot. The Frenchman grunted with pain. Thiriou released his hold on Dirk and the boy slid to the ground where he lay, gasping like a landed fish. Julie scrambled across to him. She lifted his head into her lap and stroked his hair. "Oh, Dirk," she mumbled. Dirk grinned weakly. He tried to speak but the words contorted into a garbled croak. One hand reached up to hers and pressed it tightly against his cheek.

Hayes, meanwhile, had dragged the astonished Reynouw to his feet and was proceeding to beat him mercilessly. "Get up," he bellowed, when the man collapsed for the third time beneath the onslaught. "Get up, you misbegotten son of a sow."

But Reynouw could not get up. He lay in the dirt, his face swollen and bloodied, whimpering like a beaten dog. Hayes hauled him to his feet again. He would have continued the punishment but Julie had had enough.

She went across and laid a hand on his arm. "Please, Weibbe, please, no more. You'll kill him."

The sound of her voice seemed to bring the soldier out of his rage. "Serve the scoundrel right!" he said, and he let Reynouw fall to the ground. His blue eyes softened as he turned to look at Julie.

"Did he hurt you, *kindje*?" She shook her head, but her trembling chin betrayed her. He held out his arms to her and she went into them like a child. In his warm, fatherly embrace her fear and revulsion slowly evaporated.

Hayes wanted to have both the Frenchmen flogged, and Dirk — gentle, good-natured Dirk — was so angry he offered to do the job himself. Surprisingly, it was Julie who saved them. Despite her fury she found, in the end, that she did not have the stomach for seventeenth century justice. She argued that Reynouw, at least, had been punished enough already — he would carry the marks of Hayes's beating for the rest of his life — and to flog him publicly would only cause bad feeling amongst his compatriots. With the threat of another attack still hanging over them, a divided camp was the last thing they could afford. A little reluctantly, Hayes agreed with her and the matter was allowed to rest. Outwardly at least, Reynouw appeared to have learnt his lesson, but he was not one to forgive or forget and Julie had an uncomfortable feeling they had not heard the last of him.

The following day, however, all personal grievances were forgotten in the face of a more deadly conflict. Dirk, who was on lookout duty, carried a warning back to the camp at first light. "Boats," he said; "two of them: about thirty men I'd say, and approaching fast.

And it looks as though they've left the women behind this time."

The response was instantaneous. Breakfast was laid aside, chores abandoned, late sleepers were dragged from their beds. The whole camp prepared itself for battle. There was neither panic nor confusion: Weibbe Hayes could be proud of the discipline he had imposed on his little band. Everyone knew what his job was and prepared himself swiftly and efficiently to do it. Julie was keen to go with them but Hayes stopped her. "No, *kindje*, not this time. You are needed here."

"I'm not afraid," she lied. "I've fought before; I can do it again."

But he shook his head. "I do not doubt your courage, child. But this time there will be other work for you. They have guns. There will be men wounded — badly. Someone must care for them."

Julie had not thought of that. Her blood ran cold. She was no nurse; she had never doctored anything more serious than a grazed knee. Weibbe Hayes saw her consternation and patted her on the shoulder. "Aris will be here with you. He'll show you what to do."

"Aris!" She fought back hysterical laughter. In her overwrought state, the idea of a barber wielding his razor like a scalpel over the wounded seemed insanely funny, until she realised that that was exactly what did happen — Maistre Franz had been not merely the barber but the surgeon-barber.

Aris put an arm around her shoulder and squeezed her reassuringly. "Don't worry about her, Weibbe. She'll be safe with me. And the predikant can help us too."

The predikant didn't look as though he'd be much help to anyone. His features were grey with terror and his gaunt, black-clad figure looked more like an angel of death than a consoler of the wounded. I'd hate to come to and find that face staring down at me, thought Julie. She looked slowly round Weibbe Hayes's little army, from one to the other of these men she had come to know so well. Some were grinning, some seemed to be praying — Dirk's right hand clutched his rosary through the fabric of his shirt — but in each pair of eyes the same message was written. This was their moment of truth. The skirmishing was over; today's fight would be to the death. And their opponents had all the guns.

Julie resigned herself to the unavoidable. "Very well," she said, "I'll stay here and help Aris."

"Good girl." Hayes turned back to his men. "Well, shall we go?"

Without a word they shouldered their weapons and followed him down to the beach. Julie watched them go, her eyes fixed on Dirk's back. She pressed one clenched fist against her breast as though she too held a hidden rosary. "Look after him," she whispered. "Oh, Mother of God, protect him."

13

AS SOON as the soldiers were out of sight Julie and Aris went back to the little fort and began the task of converting it into a hospital. They set up a rough operating table and tore up all the linen they could find to make bandages. Aris laid out the crude instruments he had made and Julie shuddered as she watched him sharpen them. This whole adventure was taking on the aspect of a horror movie. They had no medicines, no dressings, and of course nothing even approaching anaesthetic. And when she offered to boil his instruments for him, Aris looked at her as though she were a little strange. She hoped fervently that if any operations were needed she wouldn't be expected to assist in them.

Predikant Bastiensz hovered over them as they worked, fussing and fretting and generally getting in the way. He seemed convinced that this ordeal was a punishment sent by God and besought the Almighty loud and long to "turn aside from Your most sinful people the might of Your righteous anger". To Julie, the idea of

Jeronimus Cornelisz as an instrument of divine wrath appeared faintly blasphemous but Bastiensz seemed to find nothing incongruous in the notion. From the beach they could hear the noise of the battle. At first it was only shouting, a cacophony of angry voices that rose to a crescendo and died away again as the two sides came to grips, but presently there came the sound they had been dreading: the spine-chilling crackle of musket fire. It was followed by an eerie silence; then the shouting started again. Julie could bear it no longer. "I'm going to see what's happening," she said, and she set off for the beach as fast as she could.

"Be careful," Aris yelled after her, but he did not try to stop her.

Before she had gone a hundred paces she met Otto Smit coming the other way. He was running and his face looked haggard. "We've got wounded," he panted. "They're bringing them up now."

She stopped in her tracks. "I'll tell Aris. You go back and help them. How many?"

"Four," he said. "Three of them are not too bad but Dirk's got a blast in the chest. He's coughing up blood."

"*Dirk!*" It was though she had been struck. "Dirk! Oh my God!" She turned and fled back to the fort. "Aris, Aris, Dirk's been hit!"

She was shrieking uncontrollably. Aris grabbed her by the shoulders and shook her. "Stop it! Stop it Annetje! You won't do him any good that way."

With great effort she managed to pull herself together.

"That's better. Now, let's take it calmly and see what needs to be done. How many others are there?"

"Three," she gulped. "But Otto said the others weren't as bad."

She stood in trembling silence as the casualties were carried in. Her eyes searched each blood-stained form in turn, but when the last man had been laid on his makeshift bed she still hadn't recognised Dirk. Could Otto have been wrong? Hardly daring to hope, she approached the last bed. The man lay on his back, breathing in a harsh, gurgling rattle. The front of his shirt was soaked in blood and more of it dribbled in a scarlet froth from the corner of his mouth. Julie looked down into his face. It was the gunner, Jan Dircxsz. Relief flooded through her, followed by an equally overwhelming sense of guilt. She knelt beside him and wiped the blood from his lips. He smiled at her. His throat moved as though he were trying to speak, but then he coughed, and a gush of blood flowed over the smile and washed it away. For a moment he struggled weakly and his eyes stared, like those of a man choking, before they closed again and his breathing settled back into its ominous rattle.

Julie looked helplessly at Aris. He had cut away the tatters of cloth from the chest and was examining the bloody mess left by the shot. He shook his head slowly. "The lungs are full of blood," he said.

Julie felt panic rising inside her. "But surely there must be something . . . ?"

Again Aris shook his head. "He is not in pain. Stay with him, comfort him, bandage his chest if you like. But there is nothing I can do for him. I must see to the others."

She understood, but it did not help her. Jan was dying and she could not erase the feeling that it was she who had killed him, condemned him in that involuntary moment of thankfulness when she saw it was he and not Dirk who lay before her. As gently as she could, she bandaged his wounds and sat beside him, holding his hand and wiping away the blood that continued to trickle from his mouth.

Through the fog of her misery she could hear Aris ministering to the others. Two of the soldiers who had stayed to help him held his patients down while he worked on them. The screams of the wounded men were the sounds of which nightmares are made. Julie wanted to run. She willed Aris desperately to stop, thankful now that Jan was beyond his attentions. She raged at him in her mind. How could he do it? What kind of callous monster was he? Nothing, not even the saving of life, could justify the inflicting of that kind of pain.

When at last it was all over she turned to look at Aris. He was sitting on the wall, his face buried in his hands; all she could see of his head was a tangle of thick, brown curls; and he was shaking like a leaf. She realised then what his single-mindedness had cost him. Her dying gunner had lapsed into unconsciousness so she left him and went to Aris. She put a hand on his shoulder. "I'm sorry," she said. He turned to her with a muffled groan and she took him in her arms and let him cry.

Weibbe Hayes came up from the beach. He went from one to the other of the wounded men and then he came over to Aris. "You've done a good job, lad."

The boy lifted his head; his eyes were still glazed with horror. "No more," he whispered. "Never again. Don't ever ask me to do it again."

"This was the first time?"

He nodded.

Hayes put both hands on his shoulders and looked him hard in the face. "I shall not need to ask. You have done your duty; when the time comes you will do it again. We are grateful to you, *Maistre* Aris."

Aris Jansz stared at him open-mouthed. The title *Maistre* was accorded by custom to a ship's surgeon; it was never used to address a young, half-trained assistant. For a moment he sat unmoving; then a deep shudder ran through his body. He stood up. Tears still streamed down his cheeks but his shoulders were straight and his face held a new strength and dignity. "Thank you, Weibbe. Have you others in need of my care?"

Hayes shook his head. "Not for the time being."

Julie said: "Weibbe, what's happening down there?"

"Nothing at the moment," he told her. "The mutineers have withdrawn to their boats." He saw the hope that sprang to her face and hastened to quench it. "It's only a temporary lull. They've retired to reload their muskets. They'll be back."

"Did you get any of them?"

"No." Suddenly he looked very tired.

Fear stirred inside her. "It's bad isn't it?"

"*Ja, kindje,* I can't pretend otherwise. We have no answer to their guns. If ... when they attack again we shall have to fall back on the fort and try to engage them at close range. As long as they can fire and retreat at will they can pick us off like rooks in a cornfield."

"How much ammunition do they have?"

"More than enough." He rose to his feet wearily. "I must go back. They will be needing me down on the beach."

142

Julie resumed her vigil by the dying Jan Dircxsz. Was this what lay in wait for all of them? she wondered. She remembered the threat made to Dirk by Jacop Pietersz: 'You will wish you had died with your companions'. Was the time coming when they would all envy this man his death? Jan was still coughing blood and drifting in and out of consciousness. Bastiensz was praying with him, but his gaunt visage and doleful voice seemed more calculated to terrify than to comfort. She took Jan's hand and he moved his head towards her and smiled again. His fingers closed feebly around her own. She sat down beside him.

She had barely settled herself when there was a shout from the beach — a wild, incoherent yell that echoed across the island. Another voice took up the cry and another and another. "Come on," said Aris. He grabbed her hand and, without pausing for thought, they both ran for the beach. As they drew nearer the shouting swelled and crystallised into intelligible words: a single phrase that was chanted over and over again till it rang out like a tocsin.

"*Zeil in zicht! Zeil in zicht!*"

Breathless, they came to the edge of the cliffs and stood there looking at a miracle.

There are few sights more beautiful than a square rigger under full sail, but the sleek, swan-like yacht gliding towards High Island was a vision from heaven. The beleaguered defenders nearly went mad with joy. "It's the *Sardam*," shouted those who recognised her. "God be praised, it's the *Sardam*." They yelled and cheered and wept and waved their pikes in the air and cavorted on the sand, like children released from school. Gyjsbert Bastiensz, who had followed Aris and Julie from the fort, fell to his knees, overcome with emotion; the others, as their voices and energy gave out, joined him one by one in offering prayers of thanks for their deliverance.

Dirk rushed up the rocks to Julie and, catching her up in his arms, whirled her round and round in a crazy waltz. "We're saved," he chanted, "we're saved, we're saved, we're saved." He slapped Aris on the back and Aris hugged Julie and they all clung to one another, laughing and crying and exhausted with relief.

It was Weibbe Hayes who brought everyone down to earth. After one wild moment of euphoria he was back in command again. "The boat!" he barked. "Otto, Jan, Dirk: come with me. We've got to get to that yacht before Pietersz does!" With the three men at his heels, he took off across the island for the beach where they kept their little yawl.

Julie turned her eyes back to the mutineers. They too had seen the ship but there was no sound of cheering from either of their boats. They had drawn together, apparently in conference, and presently one of the boats, with eleven men on board, set off in the direction of the yacht, while the other pulled back towards *Batavia*'s Graveyard.

Otto and Jan were already running after Hayes. Dirk caught Julie's arm. "I must go," he said, kissing her. "If they reach *Sardam* first we're lost." As he ran to join the others, he called over his shoulder, "I'll be straight back. And don't worry — we'll beat them."

Julie and Aris made their way back to the fort. It seemed deathly quiet after the excitement on the beach. The three lesser casualties, exhausted after their ordeal under the knife, were sleeping peacefully. Jan still clung to life. His mutilated chest rose and fell with grim regularity and air gurgled in and out of his torn lungs like water through a pump. Julie sat down to wait. The first flush of excitement had begun to ebb and she was starting to feel afraid again. Surely they could not lose now? Surely, if there really was a God, He would not dangle deliverance before them like this and then snatch it away again at the last minute? Oh, what was going on out there? Why didn't Dirk come back?

It seemed an age before she heard his footsteps on the path. He was running hard. She scrambled to her feet and looked over the wall. One glance at his face told her all she needed to know. She threw herself over the wall and into his arms. He held her tightly, his whole body fierce with joy, and it was some time before he could speak; but at last he led her back into the fort and, sitting down with her and Aris, told them the whole story.

In the end it had been no contest. Weibbe Hayes, with a small boat and deep water in which to manoeuvre, had sped along the northern coast of High Island like a flying fish, while the mutineers, hampered in the shallows with their deeper draft, had floundered and struggled for every mile. The *Sardam*, meanwhile, had anchored off the island and put a landing party ashore. Hayes had met them on the beach.

Dirk described the historic meeting. Not surprisingly, Pelsaert had been suspicious at first, but the urgency of the four men had soon convinced him of their truthfulness and the gravity of the situation. After a hasty discussion the landing party had gone back to their yawl and Hayes and his men had begun the long haul back to their own island.

"And then the excitement really started," said Dirk. "No sooner had *Sardam*'s boat slid into the water than the mutineers' craft rounded the easterly point and there was a frantic race to see who would reach *Sardam* first."

"But Pelsaert won."

"Oh yes, comfortably. He had quite a head-start. He was on board waiting for them when they rowed up. There was a lot of arguing and the mutineers waved their guns around a bit but in the end they must have surrendered for they threw their weapons into the sea before climbing aboard. I should think they're all safely in irons by now."

Weibbe Hayes returned to a hero's welcome on Soldiers Island. The men who had waited on the beach to greet him carried him shoulder high back to the camp. They plied him and his little crew with wine and gin and made them recount over and over again everything that had happened: what Weibbe had told the Commandeur; what Pelsaert had said to him; what he intended to do about the mutineers. They discussed with glee the probable fate of Jeronimus Cornelisz, and Julie, listening to their predictions, found herself glancing uneasily in the direction of the other fort and wondering what thoughts were running through the minds of the two prisoners. Knowing what she now did of seventeenth century justice, she wouldn't have cared at all to be in their shoes.

Later that evening Hayes and the predikant took Cornelisz over to the *Sardam*. Everyone was glad to be rid of that evil, brooding presence. It was as though a curse had been lifted from the island and they could breathe more easily again. Weibbe Hayes returned from the yacht with a cornucopia of forgotten luxuries, including fresh fruit, and that night they all feasted like kings. Three months of hardship and anxiety were washed away with kegs of wine and flagons of gin and though the sound of their merrymaking must have wafted across to the *Sardam*, if Pelsaert guessed what was going on he made no move to stop it.

Gyjsbert Bastiensz had elected to remain on board the yacht — but nobody missed him. His disapproving presence would only have put a damper on the celebrations. The drinking and singing went on until well into the night and even Dirk, his painful promises of two weeks ago completely forgotten, joined in with gusto. Only Julie remained a little aloof. For her, deliverance had only brought a new set of problems. She sat quietly by the side of Jan Dircxsz and told him everything that had happened. Such was his excitement at the news, his eyes glowed like coals in the pallor of his face and he squeezed her hand to show he understood, even though he could not speak. She wondered if he knew he was dying and raged inwardly at the cruel chance that had struck him down in the very moment of victory. Yet all the time a tiny part of her gave thanks that it had been him and not Dirk.

He died in the early hours of the morning, quietly and without a struggle. Weibbe Hayes, doing the rounds of the camp, found Julie crying beside his body. He led her gently back to the fire, made her drink a tankard of mulled wine — a present from Pelsaert's private stock — and sat without speaking, while she poured out her grief and guilt. When she had finally cried herself out he wiped away her tears and sent her off to bed. Despite her anxieties it was not long before she fell asleep; her last recollection was of Weibbe's blue eyes twinkling down into her face and his big, confident hand wrapped consolingly around her own.

14

BEFORE DAYBREAK a yawl arrived from *Sardam* bearing no less a visitor than the Commandeur himself. Having obtained from his prisoners some idea of the bloodshed and butchery that had occurred during his absence, he was planning a dawn raid on *Batavia*'s Graveyard to arrest the remaining mutineers.

He asked for ten soldiers to accompany him. There was no shortage of volunteers and from them Weibbe picked the ten he considered suitable, including Jan Carstensz and the trumpeter Claas Jansz, who both had private scores to settle. As they were leaving he asked the Commandeur if he would take Annetje with him also. He explained her circumstances and stressed her need for protection and female company.

Julie panicked when she heard them discussing her. She was terrified at the thought of leaving Dirk and finding herself once more exposed to the curiosity of strangers. She flew to him for reassurance, but to her dismay he agreed with Hayes.

"He's right, my love. Much as I'll miss you, I'd be happier to see you in Commandeur Pelsaert's care. These men are soldiers, and they haven't had a woman in months. How long do you think it will be before some of them begin to get the same ideas as Reynouw?"

"But, Dirk..."

"Besides, think of Weibbe. As long as you stay here you're his responsibility. Don't you think he's had enough to worry about?"

She wanted to argue, but she knew he was right. Her position here was a delicate one. To remain when there was no need for it would be to invite trouble and put an additional burden on a man who had already done so much for her. Reluctantly, she agreed.

In the end it was Pelsaert himself who dispelled her fears. He took both her and Dirk aside to question them and, instead of the martinet she had been expecting, she found him an understanding and compassionate friend. He asked her very gently about everything that had happened and when he discovered that she really could not remember anything from before the night Dirk had found her, he assured her nobody would press her any further. Dirk told him briefly of Reynouw's attempted assault and he promised her, despite her protestations, that the perpetrator would be brought to justice. "And you have nothing more to fear, little one," he said, patting her on the shoulder. "You are under my protection now, and when we get to *Batavia*'s Graveyard Lucretia will look after you."

Lucretia! The name brought back to her the leonine features of Jeronimus Cornelisz and she shivered. She wondered if anyone had told the Commandeur what had happened to Lucretia Jansz during his absence.

There was no resistance from the men of *Batavia*'s Graveyard. The fight had gone out of them. Cowed and fearful, they allowed themselves to be rounded up like sheep and when Julie came ashore she could hardly believe that these were the same ferocious pirates of the previous day. Only their 'uniforms' gave them away: the boastful, gold-braided coats of scarlet *laken*, which now seemed almost pathetic in their splendour. All they had been good for in the end was to distinguish the guilty from the innocent, for the few untainted survivors, who had been kept alive to serve their brutal captors, were conspicuous in their rags. Amongst this latter group was Claas: gaunt, ragged, hungry-eyed. When he saw Julie he wept with fear, convinced she was going to denounce him, but she set his mind at rest. A few weeks ago she would cheerfully have scratched his eyes out; now she could feel only pity. He had paid a high price for his life.

And there were the women. Outwardly they appeared unharmed, but there was something in their eyes that would haunt Julie for the rest of her life. Of all the horrors experienced on these islands, there could be nothing, she thought, to equal the plight of these helpless women, tossed like playthings from one brutal pair of hands to another.

Anneken Bosschieters, weeping now in the arms of her Jan, Claas Jansz's Tryntgien and her sister Zussie: they had been used, all three, as common harlots. For Lucretia and Judith Gyjsbertsz the ordeal had been perhaps a little less terrible. They had been forced to submit to only one man and in Judith's case the union had been dignified, outwardly at least, by the name of marriage. Nevertheless they had been shamefully abused and to Julie's mind the idea of Cornelisz as a lover was even more repugnant than the thought of him as a murderer. It was easy to see why he had picked Lucretia, and why he had kept her for himself. She was beautiful: small and slender, with a complexion that even three months of wind and sun had not been able to destroy. And surely, thought Julie, there must have been Spanish blood somewhere in her background, for her hair was as black as coal and her eyes were a pure Castillian blue.

Of all the women, she was the one who still retained both pride and dignity, as though the abuse inflicted on her body had been only an outward thing and had never touched the woman underneath. She greeted Pelsaert with the aplomb of a grand lady entertaining in a mansion on the Herrenstraat, and to Julie she opened her heart with sympathetic concern. She took the girl into her tent, found her new clothes from the finery Cornelisz had heaped upon her, and defended her fiercely from all those who wanted to ask her awkward questions. Under her wing Julie felt safe. Discarding the precocious maturity she had been forced to adopt, she clung to the older woman like a child to its mother and Lucretia, understanding, was content to let her do so.

The prisoners, with the exception of Jeronimus, were removed to a hastily constructed gaol on Seals Island, from whence they could be fetched as needed for questioning. For the Captain General, other arrangements had to be made. Even in irons, he was too dangerous, in Pelsaert's view, to be left with the others. For him they devised a special prison on *Batavia*'s Graveyard; a small, windowless roundhouse, built of coral slabs after the manner of Weibbe Hayes's forts. They placed it as far as possible from the camp, on the bleak sandspit that formed the easternmost point of the island. It was a desolate spot and a cheerless shelter, but nobody wasted any sympathy on its occupant.

Captivity had not improved Jeronimus. He stormed; he threatened; he persisted in maintaining his innocence — shovelling his dirt, as Pelsaert put it, onto those who were dead and could not defend themselves. He browbeat his accusers with violent oaths and raging, amber eyes and swore a hideous vengeance on them all. Even his guards were afraid of him.

The trials began. Julie kept well away from them. She knew Dutch law allowed for torture, and she knew it would probably have to be used if they were to get the truth from these men. She had little sympathy for the mutineers, but she did not wish to see or hear what was going on in the council tent. She remembered Daniel Cornelissen and could imagine it very well for herself.

The examinations went on for ten days and on the seventh she was reunited with Dirk. He and Aris, together with Cornelis Jansz, the young assistant who had escaped from Seals Island, were brought over to give evidence against their attackers. Julie was overjoyed to see him and he brought her some interesting news concerning Jean Reynouw. It seemed the Frenchman had finally made his bid for revenge against Weibbe Hayes and it had recoiled on him badly. It happened, he told her, when Pelsaert sent a party to Soldiers Island to fetch water. Anneken and Zussie had gone with them. They had been delayed there overnight by bad weather and the following morning Reynouw accused Hayes of sleeping with Zussie. "Of course they both denied it," said Dirk. "Well, they would, wouldn't they? Everyone believed them; but instead of backing down, Reynouw tried to improve matters by suggesting that Zussie was no better than a common prostitute and that half the camp had been under her skirts that night, including himself. You can imagine the uproar it caused." He chuckled. "Our Commandeur is rather touchy about matters like that. When these trials are over and he has time to concern himself with less urgent matters Master Reynouw may well find himself scraping a few barnacles off *Sardam*'s keel."

Julie frowned. "What did you mean: 'They would, wouldn't they?'? You're not suggesting it might be true?"

He grinned. "I'm not suggesting anything. Weibbe would never force a woman, but he's no monk. If it was offered to him I'll wager he wouldn't refuse it."

"But he wouldn't lie about it. Not Weibbe."

"Why not? What damn business was it of Reynouw's anyway? Besides, Zussie's a married woman. Imagine the scandal if it was found she'd been sharing her favours." He laughed at Julie's shocked expression. "Don't waste your sympathy on Reynouw, my love. Rightly or wrongly, he got exactly what he deserved."

"I suppose so." A sudden thought occurred to her and she said mischievously: "Your name didn't happen to be on his list did it?"

"My name? Good God, no. What do you take me for?" He looked quite offended but, when he saw she was only teasing, added more candidly: "Even if I'd wanted to, half those men are riddled with the pox; you'd have to be a fool to take their leavings."

"My faithful hero!" she giggled, and fled, squealing, as he chased her along the beach with a handful of wet seaweed. There was an energetic tussle as he tried to stuff it down the back of her neck; then he scooped her up in his arms and ran into the water with her. She shouted "Put me down, put me down" and pummelled him about the shoulders, but when he pretended to drop her she shrieked even louder and clung on for dear life, with her arms twined about his neck. Laughing, he carried her back to the shore and kissed her soundly on the lips before putting her down. As they walked hand in hand back to the camp, still laughing and giggling together, she realised just how great a burden had been lifted from their shoulders. This was the first time in their relationship that they had been free to behave as normal teenagers.

The grim, judicial process ground to a conclusion. Cornelisz resisted to the bitter end. Slippery as an eel, he lied, prevaricated, told half-truths, and finally confessed everything, only to retract it again twenty four hours later. In desperation Pelsaert called the entire community together, accusers and accused alike, and in Jeronimus's presence read out the charges. When the Captain General again disputed them, Pelsaert called on the other prisoners to confirm their testimony, reminding them of the noose already around their own necks and the divine judgement which they would shortly have to face. To a man they swore, on the salvation of their souls, that every accusation against Cornelisz was justified.

Abandoned by even his own accomplices, Jeronimus finally capitulated. He made a full, public confession, admitting that all his denials had been lies, made in an effort to save his own skin. Furthermore, he expressed sincere repentance for what he had done and asked for a few days' grace in order to be baptised and make his peace with God.

At last the terrible affair could be brought to an end. Pelsaert read out the sentences. The eight ringleaders would be taken to Seals Island and there *"punished on the gallows with the cord until death shall follow"*. Nine others would be kept in chains and tried later in Batavia. The lesser offenders, among whom Claas and Jean Reynouw were named, would retain their liberty for the time being, provided they gave no trouble.

The executions were set for the first of October — three days away — time enough for the Captain General to put his spiritual affairs in order. It seemed however that Jeronimus had other plans. The very next day he slipped two letters to one of the understeersmen. They were addressed to relatives in Holland and contained all the old protestations of innocence and accusations of false testimony. By now even the tolerant Pelsaert had reached the end of his patience. He sent for his mendacious prisoner and told him exactly what would happen to him if he did not give them, once and for all, the straight, unvarnished truth. Under this threat Jeronimus backed down and repeated his confession of the previous day.

Yet less than six hours later he was recanting again; railing and storming at the predikant and swearing that God himself would work a miracle to save him from his executioners. Then he attempted suicide. What he actually swallowed nobody ever found out, but it gave him such a bellyache that the whole camp was awakened in the early hours of the morning by his roars of agony. Eventually he begged his captors for an antidote and they dosed him up with a concoction called Venetian Theriac. This saved his life, but his guards spent an exhausting night, having to drag him repeatedly in and out of his prison so that he might void his misused bowels. As Pelsaert dryly remarked, his miracle appeared to be working as well from below as from above.

The following day was Sunday. Pelsaert ordered that the condemned men should be brought to hear the sermon. Jeronimus refused to come. He told the men who were sent to fetch him exactly what they could do with their sermon and their predikant and expressed a wish that the devil, if he existed, might take the lot of them. This blasphemy seemed to shock his judges almost as much as his murders had. There was no further mention of a belated baptism for the sinner, and when on the following day fierce winds and high seas prevented a crossing to Seals Island, some of the sailors commented that it appeared even Hell didn't want him.

Finally time ran out for Jeronimus Cornelisz and his accomplices. On Tuesday, the second of October, the wind and the seas abated. The boats were made ready for the crossing. The camp was in a state of high excitement. Everyone, it seemed, was going to watch the hangings, and prepared themselves as if for a picnic. Julie was horror-stricken; she turned to Dirk for consolation, but even he seemed caught up in the air of carnival.

"How can you?" she demanded. "I thought you didn't believe in seeking vengeance."

He stared at her in astonishment. "This isn't vengeance; it's justice. Don't tell me you feel sorry for them!"

"Of course not," she said. "But to watch it ... to make an entertainment of it!"

"Why, what's wrong with that?" He seemed genuinely puzzled. "Don't people watch executions in your time?"

"We don't have them," she said.

"What do you mean; you don't have them?"

"We don't hang people."

"Not even murderers?"

She shook her head.

"Then what do you do with them?"

"We keep them in prisons."

He looked flabbergasted. "For the rest of their lives? I think I'd rather be dead."

An uneasy silence fell between them. "I don't have to come, do I?" she asked eventually.

"No, of course not, but ..." He hesitated, before adding, "I think perhaps you should."

"Why?"

He shrugged, awkwardly. "Well, it's only a feeling; probably nothing will happen, but Seals Island was where we met, where it all started. Perhaps ... "

"You mean I might be able to get back?"

"I don't know," he said. "I told you it was just a feeling. but I think at least we should try."

She was trembling; a mixture of hope and anxiety. He put an arm round her shoulder. "Will you come?"

She nodded. "If you promise I won't have to watch."

"I promise," he said. "We'll go and sit by the lake until it's all over."

They stood together staring over the water to Seals Island. Terns wheeled and swooped across the bone-white coral, their cries like the echoes of souls in purgatory. On the ridge, men were putting the finishing touches to the scaffold. She shivered. Once, in another life, she had gazed at that same spot from the deck of *Salamander*. There had been a marker-post there then, etched against the sky in silhouette: she remembered that, in her fancy, she had actually imagined it as a gallows. She felt Dirk's arm tighten affectionately around her shoulder. What was she to do? She yearned for her home and family and the security of familiar surroundings, but how could she leave Dirk? If she went back she would never see him again, for in her twentieth century world he had been dead for three hundred years.

15

THE LITTLE BASIN had never looked more peaceful. The shallow water of the lake twinkled in the sun and ripples scurried across the surface, fanned by a lively breeze. Salt glittered like quartz on the damp sand and tiny crabs scuttled in and out amongst the coral flags. It should have been a haven of tranquillity, but all its beauty could not deaden the sounds of what was happening nearby. In the shadow of the gallows the mutineers had turned on their leader. They accused him of seducing them into crime and begged the executioners to hang him first so that they might witness his punishment before they died. "Revenge!" they shouted. "Revenge!" Jeronimus shouted back at them, and the sounds carried across the island with hideous clarity.

Julie buried her head against Dirk's chest and he held her tightly until there was silence again. At last she said: "Is it finished?"

He nodded. "I think so. Would you like me to go and look?"

She clung to him. "No, don't leave me."

He held her without speaking and stroked her hair, almost absent-mindedly. The rhythmic motion of his hand was soothing, and gradually the tension went out of her. She sighed. "I used to think I was so tough. I'm not very brave really, am I?"

"Of course you are. You fought as fiercely as any of us; and who was it sat with Jan Dircxsz all those hours while he was dying? You've been a heroine, Julie; you should hear Weibbe Hayes sing your praises; and he doesn't know the half of it."

"What do you mean?"

"Well, it's been worse for you than for any of us, hasn't it? We at least know where we came from and how we came to be here; and soon we shall be going home. But for you... Oh, Julie, I'm sorry. I really thought I could find a way home for you. I thought when we got here ... But nothing's happened, nothing's changed. Are you very unhappy?"

No, thought Julie, no, I'm not, and the realisation surprised her. She wriggled into a more comfortable position and stretched her legs out before her. She was wearing her own clothes again and they felt familiar and comfortable. She twisted her head to look up into Dirk's face.

"It's funny, Dirk, a week ago, even an hour ago, I'd have given anything to go home, but now, here with you... Did you know Lucretia has offered to take me into her own home when we get back to Holland?"

His eyes shone. "Oh, Julie, I'll make you happy, I swear I will. I'll come and visit you whenever my ship is in. I'll bring you ribbons for your hair and treasures from the Orient. And when I am free of my

161

apprenticeship I'll leave the sea and marry you. I'll be the best carpenter in Amsterdam and you'll be the most beautiful lady. And when I'm rich I'll buy you a home on the Nieuwendijk and we'll fill it with children: five boys for me and five girls for you and . . . and you shall have two maids to do all the work for you!"

"Oh, Dirk," she was helpless with laughter, "ten children! I shall grow fat and ugly bearing them all and then you will not love me any more."

He leaned over and kissed her solemnly on the tip of her nose. "You will never grow fat or ugly and I shall always love you."

He had several plucked strands of the green, spongy creeper that grew across the bank, and was weaving them into a wreath. Julie watched him curiously. "What are you making?"

He held it out to her. "A courting garland. If we were in Amsterdam I would court you properly. I would come creeping to your house at night and hang this on your door. And if you loved me you would tie your ribbon around it and leave it there for all the world to see."

"And if I didn't love you?" she teased.

He looked sad. "Then you would fling it into the street and I would be desolate. I would probably throw myself in one of the canals."

"Ha," she said. "You, who were not born to drown!"

They both laughed. She took the twist of greenery from him and sat with it in her lap, fingering it contentedly. "But I have no ribbon," she said. "How shall I answer you?" And then she had a brain wave. She pulled the lace from one of her sneakers. "Give me your hand." He held out his right hand and she wound the lace around his wrist and tied it. "There. Since I have no door to hang it on, you will have to wear it yourself. Unless of course you did not really mean it. In which case you will throw it away and I shall be the desolate one."

He leaned to kiss her. "Oh Julie." His cheek was wet against hers and she realised he was crying: Dirk, who had never shed a single tear since that evening she had rescued him on the beach.

"What's wrong?" she asked, and then she realised there were tears in her own eyes as well. It stunned her: she had wept before from fear and misery and even from sheer anger, but never in her life had she ever cried for happiness.

"What a pair we are," she sniffed, laughing through her tears and mopping her eyes with her sleeve. "Anyone would think we had just said goodbye."

She snuggled into the crook of his arm and they lay side by side, watching the birds that drifted like paper arrows across the sky. "I could stay here for ever," she murmured. "It's so quiet."

"Mmmm," he agreed sleepily. Then, suddenly, he sat up. "Its too quiet. There's not a sound. Surely they couldn't have gone back without us!" He scrambled to his feet. "Come on; we'd better go and see."

His words suddenly jolted her back to reality and she remembered the circumstances that had brought them here. She thought of the sight that was waiting for them on the ridge. Dirk understood her reluctance. "I'll go first and have a look," he said. "I'll come back and tell you what's happening."

He set off round the little lake but then, on impulse, turned and came back to her. He planted a long kiss on her cheek. "For the ribbon. I shall never part with it."

Before she could answer him he was gone again. She watched with an air of idle contentment as his long legs carried him effortlessly across the damp sand and up the slope on the further side of the basin. He's beautiful, she thought. I love him. I really love him. She touched her cheek where he had kissed it, and the feel of his kiss and the image of his lean, sun-gold features remained with her long after the boy himself had disappeared from view.

She settled back to wait for him; staring lazily into the sky, with hands clasped behind her head, trying to imagine what life would be like in his Amsterdam. Would she really have ten children? Her mother had been one of ten, the eldest. She recalled family Christmases at home: all those grotty little cousins running around everywhere. No, she thought firmly; no way: not even for Dirk. She would have to make that quite clear to him.

A cloud moved across the sun and she shivered in the sudden chill. Where was Dirk? He seemed to have been gone for ages. The wind had dropped and in the stillness the waves could be heard breaking on the shore. The silence disturbed her. Even the birds had stopped crying. She began to be afraid. Where was everyone? Why didn't Dirk come back? She stood up and called his name, but there was no answer; only the echo of her own words; as though the sky itself had caught them and tossed them back again to mock her.

In the end she could bear it no longer. As she scrambled up the bank and over the spine of the island she remembered the last time she had come this way; the day the mutineers had taken Dirk. All the old nightmares came creeping back to her. From the top of the ridge she looked across the water to *Batavia*'s Graveyard. It had vanished into a fog; a solid, impenetrable fog that reached halfway across the channel and hung like a grey velvet curtain, cutting the world in two. She stood, paralysed with fear, hugging her arms around her trembling body.

And then she saw the boat. It was anchored just beyond the shallows; there were men climbing into it, and one of them was Dirk. "Wait!" she screamed, "Dirk, wait for me!" and she began to run, slipping and stumbling on the loose coral, screaming at the top of her voice, waving her arms in frantic entreaty.

No-one answered her. Nobody lifted a head or turned to look. They laughed and talked among themselves — she knew they were talking from the way they moved — but not a sound came to her ears.

Halfway down the beach she stopped, knowing with inexorable certainty that she would never reach them. They were no longer real. They were ghosts, three hundred years dead, and they had no knowledge and no memory of her. They would disappear into the mist and leave her here, alone, in limbo. She watched Dirk settle himself in the boat, and it was an agony beyond endurance. She howled like a deserted puppy. "Dirk, don't leave me. I love you, I love you."

Suddenly she saw him stiffen. His hand dropped to his right wrist and she saw her shoelace still tied around it. He looked at it and stroked it with his fingers, shaking his head as though he were trying to remember something. All at once he stood up. She saw him lift his rosary from around his neck. He held it in his hand for a moment, uncertainly; then his arm went back and he flung it towards the beach.

It landed amongst the coral, not ten paces from where she was standing. She ran towards it, but then stopped and lifted her eyes to the boat again, unwilling to relinquish even for a moment the last sight of Dirk's face. She saw him sit down. The rowers took up their oars; the boat moved silently out into the channel and the fog received it and shrouded it.

Julie stood without moving, straining her eyes into the greyness, trying to convince herself she could still see some shadowy outline. At last she knew that it was gone. She began to search for the rosary. She had marked the spot where it had fallen, but though she scrabbled like a terrier amongst the coral she could not find it. Her last security had gone. Turning, she lifted her eyes towards the ridge. Against the skyline seven scarecrow figures creaked in the rising wind; unseeing, uncaring, dead. She whimpered, and the sound was enormous in the silence.

Alone in her terror, she huddled on the coral, curled like a child in the womb, and the fog moved over her and into her and wrapped her in blankets of oblivion.

There was a hand on her shoulder.

"Julie, Julianna, wake up, love. Are you all right?"

With a cry, she reached out for the protection of that voice, and her father's arms went around her. "Oh, Julie, oh, baby, what were you doing? We thought you were hurt."

Explanation was impossible. She groped blindly for the familiar face and pulled it down to hers. "Hold me, Dad; please hold me."

The strong arms held her and rocked her and drove away the nightmare. She was sobbing like a three-year-old, but gradually her clutching hands relaxed their hold. "I'm sorry," she gulped — it was the only thing she could think of — over and over again: "I'm sorry, I'm sorry. Oh, Dad, I'm sorry."

At last she had cried herself out. She lifted her head from the security of her father's chest and peered cautiously around her. They were sitting on the beach beside her dinghy. Another boat, Ian's, was drawn up at the water's edge and the two fishermen were standing nearby, watching her with concern and bewilderment. She sniffed and tried to smile at them.

"I'm sorry. I'm all right, really I am."

"But what on earth were you doing, child?" Now that his anxiety had been laid to rest, her father sounded quite angry. "You had us worried half to death. We couldn't imagine what had happened when we got up this morning and found you missing. And then we saw you lying there on the beach. If Ian and Graham hadn't been here with their dinghy . . . "

"I know," she said. "It was stupid of me." Suddenly she saw just how stupid — and selfish — she had been. "I thought I saw smoke on the island and went to have a look. I must have fallen asleep." She shuddered suddenly and snuggled closer to him. "Oh, Dad, it was awful. I had the most terrible dreams."

He could feel her trembling. "I can well believe it," he said. "On your own here, all night; and the birds crying. It would be enough to give anyone nightmares. Especially after all that talk of ghosts yesterday." He ruffled her hair gently. "Well, love, I guess you've learnt your lesson. I won't scold you any more, but I daresay your mother will have words to say when we get back." Suddenly his face creased into a grin. "I take it you didn't find anything."

"No," she said, "nothing at all."

Ian said: "So, a ghost-hunt, eh? Me and my big mouth. Well, no harm done, but don't ever try anything like that again. These islands can be treacherous, especially at night."

"Don't worry," she promised him. "I won't."

He turned to her father. "Well, if everything's O.K. now we'll be getting back. We'll let the others know she's safe."

"Thanks," said John Dykstra. "Tell them we're on our way." He nudged Julie off his lap. "Come on, *kindje*, let's get this boat back in the water."

She didn't move. The Dutch word triggered a sudden rush of memories. They passed in a parade before her eyes: Weibbe Hayes, with his heartwarming smile and honest features; Pelsaert, gentle, tolerant, haggard with the responsibility he carried; Aris Jansz, Jan Dircxsz, Jeronimus Cornelisz. And Dirk: Dirk of the blond, spiky hair and warm, brown eyes; Dirk who had kissed her and told her that he loved her. Was it possible she had only dreamt him?

If you would be loved, then first you must love and be lovable. Dirk had taught her how to love. With his own love he had made her lovable and, dream or not, from now on his influence would colour everything she did. She looked at her father and it was as if she were really seeing him for the first time in her life.

"Dad."

He looked up.

"I've been a brat haven't I?"

John Dykstra stared at her as if his ears were playing tricks on him. A huge smile spread slowly across his face. "Yes," he said, "you've been a brat. Now, get your shoulder to that boat and let's go home and face your mother's wrath."

Together they dragged the boat down to the water. Julie's heart felt as light as a feather in the wind. Let her mother scold — she deserved it. She *had* been a brat. She could see it now and it was as though that insight had lifted shackles from her mind.

Her foot slipped on the coral. "Damn," she said. "Hang on, Dad, I've lost my shoe." She groped for it and pulled it back onto her foot. "Just wait a second till I tie it up." Her fingers fumbled for the lace — and discovered there *wasn't* one. It wasn't possible! It was coincidence. It had to be. And then she looked down at the spot where her shoe had fallen. Lying amidst the coral at her feet were three black beads. She picked them up and, closing her fingers around them, pressed them tightly against her cheek. They felt warm and solid in her hand.

The End